CW00522059

Words

A novella by

Bo Cresser

Copyright © Bo Cresser 2023
All rights reserved
ISBN 9798357108050

For Mum and Dad – this wouldn't exist without you

Here lies One Whose Name was writ in Water

– John Keats' gravestone

A young man was walking through the woods wearing a dapper, dark-grey suit and a pair of pointed, polished shoes, which were black and shiny against the matt-brown mulch of the forest floor.

A brown blur fell across his vision.

He stopped, looked down – the skeleton of an acorn now lay still on the ground. He looked up – a squirrel was sitting amongst thick oak branches, nibbling away at another prize and relishing within its grey, fat, furry body.

It was so… free–

Free from difficult decisions and self-reflection, free from existentialism and religion, free from meandering thoughts that cloud and befuddle the mind, free from insipid stories that erase the line between nut-savouring reality and… beyond, into the imagination.

It was free because its poorly-interconnected prefrontal cortex was unable to conceive such complex things. Because its pea-sized prefrontal cortex did not know that it did not know what it did not know. Because it lived a life of sensory input, a life of uninhibited impulse, a life which never questioned its own perception of reality.

The young man didn't dare move.

For a few seconds, the squirrel munched its nut to the music of nearby birdsong, a passing train, of falling orange leaves. Then the young man stretched his neck, rolled his shoulders, and tightened his blood-red bow tie. Then he continued along the leaf-layered and rotting path and the squirrel scurried away.

At the end of the woods was a concrete path which led down to several other concrete paths which led down to the platform. The young man's shoulders scuffed against the shoulders of other passengers in other dark-grey suits and red bow ties who were also shuffling down to the platform to get the same train as him in the direction he was heading along those tracks that extended to infinity.

The sky was grey, by the way. No babies. No blue.

The train arrived.

It was segmented into concatenated capsules like a multi-thoraxed centipede.

The doors opened.

The platform emptied.

The doors closed.

The train left.

Its seats were covered in a coarse dirt-blue fabric. Its windows were scarred with swirling scratches. Its surfaces were grimy with sweat and grease and breath. Two parallel bands of tungsten lighting spanned each carriage and made the thick air glow like a lantern. It was the kind of air that makes your eyes water and your lungs cramped and your head enfogged, the kind of air that leaves your fingers tainted with black.

Sturdy yellow poles divided the carriage at regular intervals and rubber teardrop nooses hung from the low ceiling. Both were slimy, barely grippable. The young man grabbed them both. Because he was standing. Because all the seats were taken. Because all the seats were full like cells in a centipede, a hundred seats in a carriage, a hundred carriages in a train, a hundred trains in…

The young man did not know what lay beyond the bounds of his weasel-like life, the burrow that it was, a life of swallowing dirt, a life of stumbling through darkness, a life of clawing at moist walls which only crumbled beneath his fingers to reveal more of the same sodden earth.

He often thought that those bounds were all there was. He had chosen them, after all. He was one of the lucky ones, after all.

Thoughts.

Words.

Images.

Every now and then, the train slowed and then stopped and then another platform would be swallowed.

After a few mindless stops, the young man noticed a small clearing amongst the standing, suit-wearing cells. He stepped into it and enjoyed the minimally more oxygenated air for a moment. Then the train shuddered and he found himself rammed against a cool and slender form. He staggered back, looked up – it was a woman of about fifty, no, younger, much younger, a woman with wrinkled skin and thin, black lips, with a freckled face and a hooked nose, with cheeks like chalk, granite for eyes, pupils as black the ocean.

She was hovering.

The train shivered and the centipede rippled and the crowed rammed him further into her. He could smell the fust of her perfume. He could hear the stillness of her breath. He could feel her coldness sapping his heat like ice or slate or a black hole.

He shoved himself away.

Shadows were cast by her swaying, swaying feet.

He struggled across the carriage, wading through that swathe of faceless bodies, drowning in the grey and swamp-like tide. The train slowed and he thanked god. The doors opened and he staggered out and coughed up a thick glob of mucus and spat it out onto the ground. He stood there, still, on the platform, breathing, heavily, as bodies pushed past him, around him, through him, as the train emptied the acidic contents of its bowels.

The young man's breathing slowed as the centipede

slithered off to find more food and the platform drained away. Then he stretched his neck, rolled his shoulders, and tightened his blood-red bow tie. Then he left the platform and rejoined the flow of bodies heading in the same direction as he was heading along a long, wide road with invisible edges.

At the end of the road was the Institute. That blocky palace. That haven of concrete and creativity.

The flow of bodies slowed as it reached the revolving doors. The young man revolved, queued inside, then he rested his hand on a reader such that a green light beeped and a pair of butterfly wings were torn apart. He stepped through them with practised urgency.

He navigated to his room in Zone Three, to his door with its peeling, red paint, its crooked number, and its corroded handle. He turned the handle and stepped inside.

It was a small room – two metres square – with a desk and a chair. He sat down on the chair, as one does. On the desk sat a computer, a keyboard, a mouse, and a thin coating of dust, its method of entrance unknown to him, for there were no windows, not one.

He pressed the spacebar on that slab of black plastic gridded with fat buttons stamped with symbols and letters and actions. The computer whirred and, as it whirred, he removed a brown notebook from his inside breast pocket and laid it out in front of him. On its lines were a litany of cranial treasures looted by his previous self, fragments of thoughts worth diamond and opium and gold.

The computer made a clicking noise and then a blank white screen popped out of its squat body. It licked its lips. The young man tasted the taste of his own lips as he stared at the pixelated screen and the pixelated screen stared back at him, at his veiny, transfixed eyes.

He closed those eyes but the screen stayed awake and a story began to emerge from its binary depths.

Why? Because the young man had started typing. He'd started typing and he was typing and he typed. He typed until his wrists began to ache and his fingers stiffened and the pads of those fingers went numb. He typed until his eardrums went numb to the continuous rat-a-tat-tat of the plastic keys, in and out, in and out, in and out.

He was like a ten-legged spider weaving an intricate web. One of the signs. One of words. One of language. A tale of monsters internal and external, of adventure and hope and tragedy and pain, poured out of his mechanical hands. It was as though he had instinctual creativity which shut down the inhibiting part of his brain and separated conscious thought from intuition by an ephemeral, partially-permeable membrane.

A few hours passed.

The door opened. A blue-jacket placed a paper bag onto his desk and then left. The young man took a sandwich out of the bag – white bread, pink ham – and ate it with one hand as he typed with the other. Then he ate the other sandwich. Then an apple. Then he dropped the paper bag into a small metal-mesh bin in the corner of the room. He kept typing.

A few more hours passed.

Every twenty minutes, he took a moment to stare at where the window should be. Every forty minutes, he rolled his shoulders and stretched his legs.

A few more hours passed.

As the timer on the screen hit thirty minutes left, the young man rounded up the novel's plot. As the timer hit ten minutes, he skimmed the thing for errors. As the timer hit one minute, without a flinch, he hit 'Enter' with the pad of an extended right pinkie. Then he typed a title, a subtitle, a dedication, a blurb, and a dozen keywords to be checked against the system. He hit 'Enter' again.

"Confirm publication?" said the screen to the man on the chair in the minuscule room. He hit 'Enter' again. For a few moments, a small ring chased its ever-fading tail. Then it disappeared, leaving a blank white screen fresh and shining, beckoning him to start anew and to fill its empty, digital pages.

But the screen would have to wait.

Zero zero.

A bell rang.

The young man straightened his blood-red bow tie. Closed and pocketed his notebook. Stood and stretched his back with a crack. Left the room. Shut the door. Followed the tide of grey-suited others down corridors and stairs and through grey butterfly barriers into the open air. Then onto the station and onto the train and off the train and back into the open air.

He wandered through the woods, his strange green haven, that miniscule green area between his station and his complex of concrete abodes. He did not see the squirrel. He stared at the sun as it set.

He left the woods and navigated the gridded paths to his block. He placed his hand on the reader.

A white ding. The door opened.

The low, cold sun was replaced by panels of bright light and harsh shadows. The shadows smelled of chemicals. The light had the texture of a moth.

Corridor. Printer. Stairs.

Another reader went ding and another door opened. The door. His door. A door.

The young man had arrived home.

The young man's home was like all the other homes run by the Institute. He closed the door and shrugged off his jacket and hung it up on a smooth silver hook. He cracked his knuckles.

"What a day," he said to his partner, who was standing at the stove, staring into a bubbling bowl of pasta, white, penne, with its oblique, open ends and faint, linear markings running lengthways and parallel all around its outside, those tiny demarcations of unintelligible purpose.

"Is that sarcasm?" she said to him as he sat down on a small stool and began to untie the laces of his shiny, black shoes.

She took the pan off the stove with the force of a strained bicep and a clenched fist. Then she turned to the small, silver sink and poured the contents of the pan into a small, silver sieve. Most of the starch-saturated water drained out in a gush. The rest of it dripped out after a moment of tossing, all while the pasta remained within that finely-hatched wire mesh of metal strands, an enclosing dome from below but one that let steam rise out from its gaping top.

She put the pan down and tipped the sieve's contents into two bowls on the table with forks beside them. The young man had undone his bow tie, untucked his white shirt, and rolled up his sleeves. He turned off the stove and they both sat down to eat the plain pasta, al dente to the bite.

"You're early," she said.

"Am I? I must have walked quickly."

She chewed another mouthful. "Perhaps I walked slowly. What did you write about today?"

"The usual."

"What's that supposed to mean?"

"You know, whatever comes into my head. You can't explain creativity."

"Sure." She nudged the large brown envelope that was resting on the table towards him, the numerals 3-1659 stamped in red ink onto the front. "I got your report from the printer."

"Thanks." He put down his fork and prised open the envelope, digging his thumb into the gap at one corner and tearing back that part of the flap, then the next part, then the next part in small, jagged semi-circles until the whole edge was open. He shoved his thumb and fingers into its throat and pulled out the enclosed document.

"How were the profits for last month?" his partner

said.

His pupils flickered over the printed page. "My historical fiction piece didn't do very well. I guess it was a bit rushed. 'Dreams in Wonderland' made a decent profit though."

"Yes, but how much did you make?"

"Huh, my comedy did pretty well. That was a short one too." He turned the page.

"Don't ignore me, darling. Can we afford the rent?"

"Hang on. I'll skip to the end. Oh, 'The Captain' did surprisingly well. I wasn't expecting that." Pause. "Now 'Death', I expected that to fly off the printers."

"Oh, for Christ's sake. Let me see that." She grabbed at the report.

"Okay, okay." He moved it out of her grasp then handed it to her slowly. "Calm down."

"It's not me who needs to calm down. It's you who needs to calm up. Let me see this report." She flicked to the end. "You're barely covering the cost of Zone Three. What have you been doing all day? Not writing, that's for sure. At least not anything anyone wants to read."

"Darling, that's not fair. I spend all day, every day, writing and I'm getting better."

"Oh, don't feed me that nonsense. Do you know what you told me last month? 'I'll get better. I promise.' The month before that? The same thing."

"Darling, just give me more time."

"You're not listening. It's been a year. A year. A

child could have gotten better than you in a year."

"That's not fair."

"Oh, we're talking about fair now. It's not that your stories are bad. It's that they don't sell. We have expenses, you know. I'm working overtime at the school because you can't even write a decent yarn. Don't talk about 'fair' with me. Why are we paying for Zone Three anyway? It's not like your writing needs high security if it doesn't even sell."

"It–"

"Yeah, yeah. I know why. Because you want to get credit for your 'art', whatever that's supposed to mean. Guess what, no one cares about your writing. I used to, but I'm not so sure anymore."

She looked around at their plastic-wood floor, their barren kitchen, the lampshadeless light. "I'm paying for it, that's for sure. Christ, am I paying for it."

She looked out of the window at the vista of grey dominoes in the dark-grey light. "We moved here for you and you're gonna need to get your act together – you're gonna need to start making some money or I'm leaving this godforsaken place."

She put down the report and resumed eating. She bit into a forkful of the starchy stuff and grimaced. "And now the pasta's cold. Nice one. It was disgusting anyway, who am I kidding."

They finished the cold pasta in silence.

Then the young man took their forks and their bowls to the sink, washed them up, and left them on the drying rack.

He sat back down, looked at the scowling face before him and then down at the splayed-out report. That was when he noticed a block of text at the very bottom of the final page–

 NOTICE TO CLIENTS. On Thursday 16th, our tri-annual, inter-zonal Inspiration Day will commence. It will be a chance for the writers of the Institute to hone their craft in an open and constructive environment. Join us on the day if you wish to participate in this opportunity. You will not be refunded for time spent not writing during the session.

"Have you seen this?" He showed it to his partner, who read it silently. "Shall I go?"

 "Well, a refund of nothing is nothing, so yes. Why not? It might even help you get your act together." She sighed, stood, and went to their room, the soft shuffling sound of her socks fading away, the door closing – she went to their room to probably read some pithy romance novel before falling into dreams of other men.

The young man aligned the edge of the report with the edge of the table.

He stood up and put the maimed brown envelope into the kitchen bin. Then he slouched down into his green, felt armchair, which moulded to his body like clay. He tried to read the book on the side table, but he couldn't. He just couldn't – his mind found more important dreams and thunderclouds to think about after every other line. He put the book down and tried jotting ideas into his notebook, but you cannot jot ideas if there are no ideas to jot. And so, he gave up. Just – stared into space, for a while… And when all he could see behind the curtains was darkness, he turned off the light, and joined her in bed.

He awoke the next morning with a soft duvet weighing down on him, listening to the sounds of his partner sitting on the other side of the bed, popping pills into her mouth and guzzling them down with water from a slender glass. He sat up and squinted at her outline in the hazy morning light, tried to make out the finer details of her form.

She stood up and went to leave but paused at the door. She opened her mouth as though to speak but closed it again. She stood still like a statue made of liquid clay. "Just try to earn some money today. Please?"

The young man nodded.

She left.

The young man's ability to write had stagnated like a swamp, brown and thick with dying life and matter. He had been pulled into a wet abyss of self-hatred and shame until a silence of thought and expression enveloped and permeated his very being.

When Inspiration Day finally arrived, he went.

He went filled with hope that it would fish him from that undeserved muck without gashing the roof of his mouth. He hoped that the worm that baited him would be a tasty one, that it would be easy to digest, and that even if there was a certain sourness – a few tangy intestines perhaps – that it would be a satisfying sourness. But most of all, he hoped to be carried over and released into clean, clean, azure water, as blue as the sky, the blue sky that is only blue because of the light reflected off blue water, or perhaps it is the other way around.

All he wanted was to find a shoal to assimilate into

with its ordered, safe, mutual passivity. He did not know which shoal he might join. He did not know whether he would be accepted or not. He did not know whether he would remain alone.

All he knew was that the corridor to Hall Two was crammed with suited bodies like a tin of kippers wrapped in grease, somehow still alive and all flapping their grey bodies so that they could be swallowed a few moments sooner by the Hall.

Hall Two. The second Hall. Second, out of many, the number of which the young man did not know nor care to know.

The young man entered.

The Hall was lit with bright white light from above, as opposed to below, because below would be irrational and disturbing. The Hall's proportions were unremarkable. There was a stage at the far end and rest of the space was filled with several hundred fold-up chairs in a neat lattice of rows and columns.

There was a large printer by the entrance which was churning out flimsy paperbacks for clients to take as they entered. The young man took one. It had the usual white cover with the title 'Love is Forever.' The young man approached and sat in an empty seat in the middle of the Hall, as instructed.

To his left sat a woman who did not even glance in his direction. In front of him was a balding crown. Then a blonde head of hair. Then a mullet. Then the young man gave up being observant and merely cast his eyes over the other few hundred heads in the formation, all framed by blood-red bow ties upon white collars within dark-grey suits.

However, the man to his right was notable because he reached out to shake his hand. This man's hand was as firm as it was hairy and shaking it was like greeting a small gorilla.

"Nice to meet you," its owner said. His voice was gruff and monotone. He had a receding hairline which was compensated for by bushy sideburns and a well-fed belly. "I'm Brian. Which Zone are you in?"

"Zone Three, you?" the young man said as he removed a thick black hair from his sore hand.

"I've just upgraded myself to Zone Seven. I must say that I'm doing rather well for myself." He smiled lopsidedly and then coughed a deep cough. "But who am I to brag? We're all professionals here." He laughed deeply. Indulgently.

The young man looked around. "Do you know why I've never been to one of these events before?"

Brian furrowed his black brow. "Well, you need to have been here for a couple of years before you're invited. I suppose the fledglings already have enough inspiration in them, eh?" He drew his elbows to his sides and flapped them up and down in a noisy impression of a small bird, then slapped his thigh with boisterous enthusiasm.

Brian's avian impression was interrupted by a crimson-clothed woman walking onto the stage, the metronomic taps of her high heels echoing around the hard room. She stopped before a lectern in the middle of the stage and the lighting dimmed, imposing silence.

The room relished in that silence.

After a few moments, a dwarfish man waddled onto the stage and handed the red woman a microphone. She held it close to her face and shouted with high-pitched glee–

"Hello!"

The loudspeakers whined like a stray dog being dismembered by harsh reality. The crowd winced as though unwillingly witnessing this self-imposed limb-chopping. Then, ingeniously, the woman on stage moved the microphone slightly further away from her face. She tapped it a few times with a few tentative pops.

The dog regrew its limbs. "Hello?"

The woman beamed like a sun. "Hello. Hello hello hello. Welcome to our third and final Inspiration Day of the year." There was cheering. Clapping. Whooping. "The fire exit is back the way you came. Please stay seated for the duration of the session etc. etc. Enjoy, stay safe, and make sure to get your…" She made a clicking noise with one side of her mouth "…creative juices flowing!"

More clapping, like a herd of penguins realising that they could whack their wet flippers together.

The woman on stage giggled for no apparent

reason, then stopped, and continued. "I suppose I should introduce myself. I'm Hanna and I am one of the more successful writers at the Institute." She smiled kindly. "Some of you will know that my latest book 'Love is Forever' has just been awarded the Most Successful Book of the Month Award, which I couldn't be more honoured to have received."

The clapping crescendoed.

"Thank you, thank you," she responded, "but there's no need to clap. However, if you do feel the need, clap for the fact that I will be your host for this morning's session of inspiration and creativity! Later on, another author, a consumer specialist, and a selection optimiser will be speaking. But let's not worry about that now. Until then, I have the honour of reading aloud some extracts from my new book. There will be group discussions so that you can learn from each other. And I'll be sure to share my very own tips and tricks to make your writing more like mine."

The crowd went wild. The young man massaged the tightness in his neck.

Then the red woman put her microphone on a stand and held up a hand for silence. "Let's read, shall we?"

There was a shuffling as people retrieved their copies and flicked to the first page.

Hanna did the same. "Make sure to look at the dedication," she said, "which reads 'Dedicated to you'. My first piece of advice is to always dedicate your work to your reader. They like that. Trust me, it will double your earnings in the blink of an eye." She blinked both of her eyes emphatically. The crowd laughed. Then she paused and beamed like a blinding star – no, like a galaxy, a galaxy with an army of glistening teeth. "Now, I'll read, shall I?"

The crowd yelled 'Yes!' in dissonant unison.

Hanna began to sprinkle her fairy dust. "Once upon a time, there was an innocent person named Nelly. She was walking to work when she saw a handsome man across the street.

"He was so handsome. He was so handsome that she couldn't help staring at him! She had to stop walking because it was so difficult to stare at him and walk at the same time. She was utterly transfixed and her heart was pounding so she knew it must be love. She was willing him to stop and look at her with every ounce of her body.

"And he did.

"He sauntered over to her side of the road. Her stomach was full of butterflies.

"'Hey,' he said.

"'Hi,' she said.

"It was love at first sight. They kissed passionately.

"Then he whisked her off into his helicopter, which was conveniently located nearby. It was New Year's Eve and had gotten dark. The sky went bright with the colours of fireworks. They sat in the safety of the helicopter and watched the fireworks together.

"'What's your New Year's Resolution?' Nelly asked

her man.

"He thought for a long, attractive moment. 'To be with you,' he said."

The crowd broke out into rapturous applause.

"Now wasn't that a blast?" she said. "Now, with the people around you, talk about the opening. Pay attention to how it makes you feel and why it makes you feel that way. Remember, you're here to be inspired, so be inspired!"

At first, the Hall was tentative and quiet but soon it burst into an enthused chatter. The young man noticed the voices behind him.

"What an introduction," one female voice said. "Especially how she begins with 'Once upon a time'. Hanna is so clever at letting readers know that they are reading a story."

"Yes, definitely," said another woman's voice. "The use of 'every ounce of her body' is clever too. I think that readers like to be reminded of old things, like the old measurements."

"Yes, you're right," said a third woman. "I also like what she did structurally by starting most sentences in the first paragraph with the pronouns 'he' or 'she'. I think that it's useful for readers to know who is doing the action in each sentence. No wonder Hanna is such a successful writer."

They all mumbled words of affirmation and started nattering once more but the young man had since zoned out. He turned to Brian and Brian turned to him.

The young man mustered his courage like mustard, like a muster of peacocks made of custard. "Brian, this might be wrong of me to say, but I – I didn't think the writing was very, well, good."

Brian opened his mouth but, before he could vibrate his vocal cords, one of the voices from behind them erupted with "How could you offend such a talented writer?!"

The young man turned around in his chair and looked at the woman who had spoken, looked at her slim face and her long, straight honey hair. "No no – you don't understand – I don't think Hanna's writing is bad–"

"That's what it sounded like to me." She spoke with the spite of a hundred honey bees attacking a wasp that had invaded her hive.

"No – I didn't mean it like that – or maybe I did, but…" He glanced at Brian. Brian was staring at him. "I just think it's a bit, you know, cheesy? And a bit cliché? And, I just don't know where the story is going – the romance has already finished by the end of the first page."

The honey woman, whose reply had been bubbling hot and sticky inside of her, suddenly let forth her viscous words. "But what about how the light imagery 'colours of fireworks' represents their burning love? What about the heartfelt and minimalist dialogue? What about the overwhelming sense of passion? The emotion conveyed is so strong!"

The young man held up his palms defensively. "You're right. You're right. Maybe I just don't know anything about love."

The woman was about to let forth that oozing flood once more when – thank god – Hanna called for attention from the front of the Hall.

But then Hanna too was interrupted for a voice from the front of the Hall yelled "I love you, Hanna!" and a small figure clambered up onto the stage. Somebody was up on the stage and was koala-ing and kissing Hanna's legs and feet.

"Oh no!" Hanna declared as two blue-jackets ran over and grabbed the struggling figure and dragged it off the stage and out through a silver door which clanged behind them with a deep resonant frequency and overtones of punishment.

With the interruption removed, Hanna smoothed out her blood-coloured dress and continued. She talked about narrative arcs and sentence construction and character creation and reader attention. There were moments of group reading and complementing alongside moments of listening and vanity. The young man did not speak much after his conflict with the woman behind him.

Near the end of her section, Hanna said "I have one more piece of advice for you all, and I hope it will make all the difference." The crowd was silent with anticipation. "Are you ready?

"Yes!"

"Are you sure?"

"Yes!"

The audience interaction was awe-inspiring.

Hanna melted. "Listen carefully. This isn't really advice. It's more of a plea. Please, please, if you take anything away from this session that we've shared together – any one thing – it's this. Always remember to write from your heart." She held her hands to where her heart should be.

The crowd went "Awwwww".

The crimson woman left the stage.

There were a few more speakers after Hanna, as expected, who talked about genre targeting and pricing automation and reading-duration maximisation. The day rolled on like a pebble propelled by a gentle stream.

Then the day ended and the crowd began to leave. The young man turned to Brian. "Brian, you're an experienced writer, right?" He nodded. "Could you tell me what you think of Hanna's writing? Is it actually good writing?"

Brian laughed. "It's not just good writing. It's great writing. Hanna just won the Most Successful of the Month Award."

The young man winced and dug around for the right words. "Yes, of course. But I don't mean its popularity. I mean the actual writing style. The literature. Is it good literature?" He held up his copy of 'Love is Forever' and it wobbled. The nosey, honey-covered woman noticed and chuckled with her companions as they strutted away.

But Brian ignored them and began to speak. "Writing doesn't need to convey some sophisticated message, if that's what you mean." He gestured to the stage which Hanna had left hours earlier but somehow still symbolised her presence. "Hanna, she's living the life. She's riding the wave of success. People love her work. They love the passion, the predictability, the permanence of its every page. They love that it's there and it knows it's there. They love that it's there for them as they read it and that it's never going to disappear like money or love or real life."

Brian rubbed his fingers; the words were powder on his fingertips. "They love the fact that even though its pages will be shredded and mulched and regurgitated, the story will still exist because it never existed at all." He shuffled further into his chair, which bent under his weight like a convex lens.

"Hanna's work makes people happy. It makes them content. Like a drug. Like bliss. It makes them feel all warm inside as though they've just swallowed a spoonful of soup that isn't metallic in their mouth, for once, that isn't either stone-cold or tastes even more metallic because of the image residing in their minds of the very coins it cost them to heat it."

He wiggled his fingers with contentment at being able to maintain such an expansive thought. He smiled, thought for a moment, and continued. "One book can last a week for one of the masses, busy as they are. If they return it to the printer, they get half that back. Buy a new one and – quod erat demonstrandum – they've got a never-ending source of euphoria. Every other line is a frisson." Brian shivered.

"Hanna's writing, what I aspire to write, and the writing of the best darn writers in this Institution, it lets people escape from the misery of their miserable lives. I like to think that it releases their minds from their bodies in this way like doves released from a magician's sleeves. With magic reduced to thievery, writers are the only ones left who can create this sparkling disbelief, who can hold up a piece of cloudy acetate to the world where it's reality that scares children into submission and keeps them awake at night."

Brian paused. The pause was for effect. "Shouldn't that be the point of writing?" Another pause. Just as effective. "Shouldn't that be the point of 'literature'?" Another pause. Longer now. More pregnant, bulging, ripe. "Shouldn't the words that we write allow our readers to voraciously, rapaciously, indefatigably consume and feed and escape and to hide away in a way that even I don't understand, that no one really understands, but just … is?"

Brian paused again. Paused as in stopped. He was done, with his speech, his monologue, his performance.

The young man's temples hurt. The bodily ones, not

the temples of long-gone religion.

He tried to stutter out a response, but he couldn't. Not for a while. He just muttered "You're right, of course, you're right," as chairs scraped and feet pattered all around them.

Then the young man pulled his small notebook from his jacket pocket. He turned it around in his hand as he heard the following words in his mind a few seconds before they emerged from his mouth. "Could you read an example of my work and tell me what you think?"

"Yes of course," Brian said, and so the young man flicked open his notebook and handed it to his newfound jury and judge.

Brian took the notebook, squinted, and read. He read on some more, then he relieved the tension in his eyes, looked up to the young man, and closed the notebook. He furrowed his brow. "I don't know how to say this, and I don't mean to be harsh, but no one's going to want to read something like that." He rubbed imaginary sleep from his eyes with his furry fingers.

"It's just depressing. It's like real life. Or it's real life for the majority of your potential readership. And illness is something that no one likes to linger on. The only way to please people's souls is by writing about things exotic and different to their cruel and miserable lives."

The young man took back the notebook. "But didn't Hanna's story begin in a city? Why is it bad when I do it?"

Brian turned further towards the young man. "Yes, but Hannah's was a city without pollution. It is as fictional as a desert oasis." His pupils constricted and dilated as he spoke. "If you want to write better fiction, read her books and try to pick up her style. Unless you're not trying to sell your work, in which case write whatever you like."

The young man pocketed his notebook. "Thank you for being honest."

Brian looked him up and down slowly and squinted. Then he leant forwards, his hairy belly peering out from between the buttons of his shirt. He was looking intensely at the bridge of the young man's nose as though he was staring into both eyes at the same time. "If you ever need help with writing, or life, go to room 6899 in Zone Nine." He shrugged. "You might find what you're looking for."

"Who's in room 6899?"

"You'll find out if you ever visit. I haven't been in a long time but I'm sure you'll be welcome." At that, Brian stood and began to saunter away. The young man joined him awkwardly, and they followed the slowly exiting masses.

That night, the young man read the rest of Hanna's book. The male character ended up having a series of affairs before dramatically apologising. Then they both lived a long life of devotion to a ripe old age. At the end of the novel, Hanna acknowledged all five of her pet budgerigars along with everyone who has and will ever read any of her books. The 'About the author' section was several pages long with her achievements.

He fed the book into his block's printer and got a small sum added to his account. But the memory of the book lingered in his mind. It was a sour memory, like vinegar.

The next day, he was sitting in room 1659, Zone Three, as he did most days, every day, and he tried to replicate what he had read: commas, speech marks, exclamation marks, full stops, word choice, sentence length, structure, plot. He was trying. He was failing. He hated himself. His words felt hollow, as though they had yet to be shaded in by a bored child, the empty spaces not filled with the dusty graphite of a soft pencil. They felt unannotated, unloved, uninterested in themselves.

It was done.

But instead of pressing 'Enter', he selected all of the text with the press of two keys and then slapped the 'Delete' key.

It was gone.

He slammed his fist down on the keyboard.

The letter 'J' popped out of its socket, scuttled across the desk and fell onto the floor.

He pictured his partner. He pictured himself telling her that he was a failure and her responding, 'I know.' He pictured the world in a thousand years with no trace of who he was, his pathetic work unread, forgotten, lost. He pictured Brian's vacant smile and

Hanna's swirling grin. He pictured the soul-sucking woman he had been rammed into on the train and he felt the feeling of knowing that he would one day possess that same vacuum, would be, was, not, never, is–

The computer screen had been smashed, somehow. The keyboard was in pieces, somehow. The mouse looked like a mouse no more. He slumped down and turned his body around and banged his head against the windowless wall.

Again and again and again…

Footsteps.

The door opened.

A man in a blue jacket grabbed him.

Hoisted him up.

Carried him out…

White room.

A man with an egg head and a porcelain suit.

"You have committed violence against the property of the Institute. The appropriate fine will be abstracted from your account in instalments. Failure to reimburse the cost of this damage will result in expulsion from all Institute facilities upon immediate effect."

When the young man saw the size of the fine, he cried. Surely a chunk of plastic couldn't cost that much? Surely a computer screen couldn't cost that much? He cried like a baby…

Home.

Plain pasta. Small portions.

"How did the writing go today?" she asked.

"Pardon?"

"How did the writing go today?"

"Oh."

"Well?"

"Yeah, it's going well."

He bent over the bowl and let the hot steam rise up to his face.

A few identical, iterative, quotidian days later, the young man was navigating to his miniscule room. Again. Like every day. Except he couldn't help but find himself distracted today, distracted by running his hands along the corridor's peeling paintwork, distracted by the soft ache in his legs upon every step, distracted by the softness of the carpet and the length of the corridors and by his own flickering, fiddling thoughts. It was so quiet.

Doors passed on either side of him.

The young man stopped.

He stopped right in front of a door such that he would only have to stoop down and peer through the keyhole to see its occupant – and before he knew it, he was peering at a thick-set man with heavy hands pummelling keys with tremendous speed. He had such drive, focus, confidence, arrogance. The young man's palms began to sweat. His bent knees shook. His head hurt. But then he managed to muster the manliness to man-up like a goddamn man and forced himself to imagine that this other man was awful, that he was writing awful fiction, that he was in awful poverty, in crippling debt, unable to feed his family, that his family were starving and had abandoned him, that all he had left was the carnal pleasure of stringing clichés and tricks and garbage phrases onto a soulless screen.

The young man felt better. He relaxed.

But even then, he couldn't imagine himself going up to that room with its coating of dust and its windowless walls. He couldn't imagine sitting down on that hard-backed chair imitating writing that he didn't like and didn't know why. He just couldn't. That was when the young man decided to go to room no. 6899.

And so up, up, up, he went.

The paintwork was neater here. The door handles had a silver shine and the doors themselves were spaced further apart. Even the lighting was brighter but also less bright, nicer. Although maybe it was just his eyes.

When the young man got to the sought-for door, he stood before it for a few seconds and stared at the silver digits screwed into it. Then, at last, he knocked. Twice.

Silence.

A strained voice broke out from within. "Come in."

The young man reached for the handle and turned it

slowly and pushed open the door.

Inside was a man covered in wrinkles sitting on a green, felt armchair. The room contained a desk and a computer and a mouse and a sofa and a grate from which cool air breezed through. Electrical heating buzzed and warmth laced the air and the whole room was engulfed in dim blue light and the smoke of burning frankincense, redolent with spice.

The young man took a step onto the pillowy carpet, crimson but purpled by the room's blue mist. "Sorry to inconvenience you. A man called Brian told me that I could come here if I needed help."

The wrinkled man rapped bony fingers against the felt armchair a few times. His suit was the same as the young man's, of course. Except the wrinkled man's suit was as smooth as scales and was fitted to his body like skin. He was a snake inside-out, his suit the soft skin of a freshly moulted serpent while the body inside resembled its shed and weathered hide.

Except the old man didn't hiss. He just looked the young man up and down with hollow eyes. Then he wafted a thin hand at the door. The young man closed it. Then he wafted his hand towards the floor. The young man sat down, cross-legged like a child and painfully like a arthritic child crawling beneath rocks, their harsh surface cutting the skin on its fragile knees and scraping scars into the tops of its feet.

The old, old man held a cup in one hand. Tea, it seemed. "Tell me…" His voice was as wrinkled as his skin. He took a sip. "What is it that you want?"

The young man stretched his back. "I want to be a better writer so that I can make more money."

Another sip of tea. "But do you want the latter or the former, friend? The latter or the former?"

"Aren't they the same?"

"No, no, no!" the wrinkled man cried. He put his tea down beside his keyboard and started gesturing violently as though his shoulders might pop out from their sockets. "You see I am rich, but I am not a good writer. I couldn't write a good yarn if you put a bullet to my head."

His yellow eyes seemed to swell as he spoke – they swelled as though aflame but flickered away each time the young man met them such that he wondered whether there was any contact at all.

"But it doesn't matter – 'why?' you ask – because I have lots of money, lots of gold little numbers in my account."

As he spoke, he enveloped them both with his words and his wisdom and unwavering flame and the young man let himself be surrounded by that blue and yellow heat.

"What you want, my friend, is to be rich, so that you don't have to worry about all this book-selling muck. You see, if you are rich, then you can write the most nonsensical literature." He nodded to his computer. "Read some of mine." But the young man remained where he sat and the text on the screen was but a blur.

"You might cry 'but I don't want to write nonsensical literature', to which I would say, 'but no one understands you, do they? If they did, you wouldn't be here.'"

So much smoke and scent and blue heat. So many flames forming one large flame. "Trust me, young man, it's all about money. Money means you don't need to worry about your writing being profitable and popular and politically correct. You've got to think economically to be a bad writer. You've got to think wealth, think interest, think smart, not hard."

He leant towards the burning frankincense and inhaled deeply. He spoke louder, now, eyes wider. "How do you get this elusive money? The answer is simple. You must venture to the City. That is where I made my fortune."

The young man picked a piece of red fluff from the soft carpet and rolled it into a tight ball. The old man leant forwards and stared into his soul with closed eyes.

"You likely lived in the City before you came here. But it is a different place now, a place of opportunity. The Economy is booming more than ever before. Poverty does funny things to the masses. It lights the fire in their bellies.

"You need to find yourself and then find your wealth. It will only take you a few days to amass enough riches to live forevermore like a fat ferret." He tapped a long index finger made of more knuckle than flesh against a hollow temple. "If you're smart."

The wrinkle-skinned man in the tailor-made suit pushed himself back into his large, soft chair and crossed his legs like a buddha. "The people who depend on you will love you more when you come home a new and richer man. But don't think about others. Think about yourself. You will be able to write whatever you wish, to unleash your creativity and form your legacy. You can be… free–

"Don't write for the unappreciative cranks of today. Write what is true. Write for the future. Write for those who will read your writing decades after your death and who will revere you, who will believe in you, who will understand you better than you could ever understand yourself.

"As you know, Institute stories are safe forever, stored in deep depths free from corruption. And the more money you pay, the safer they are. Money is the flesh that makes us up after death. Money is the charge that connects people to fame, words to meaning.

"Trust me, my friend. I may be old, but I am not foolish. This body is less strong but wiser than yours. This brain is less fresh but more filled than yours. Go to the City. Strike a deal. Return home a winner. What is there not to like?"

The young man stared at the wall. The young man stared at the floor. The young man stared at the ceiling. He did not know what to think. He did not know how to reply. All he knew was that the old man's words felt right.

So he nodded. A small nod but a significant nod. A solemn nod but a steadfast nod.

The old man smiled a toothless, gummy smile. "You must leave tomorrow morning and get the first train to the City. The driver is a friend of mine. He can recommend a place to stay."

He nodded towards the door. "Now leave me be. I have nonsense to write."

The young man stood up one leg at a time. He paused in the middle of that smoke-filled, blue-tinted room. As he went to leave, he turned around and spoke. "Thank you for helping me. I've been feeling like the world is my antagonist lately."

The old man inhaled the incense intensely once more. "We all get battered and bruised. It just takes time to learn to cover up our scars."

The young man soon discovered that packing is easier when you know how long you are going to be away. Similarly hard is telling your partner that, why, who, what, when, and how long you are going to be away.

"I'll only be a couple of days. I might even head off this morning, so I won't be here for dinner."

"Oh. Okay," she said as she swallowed her pills while sitting on the edge of the bed. She left.

The young man swallowed his own powdered capsules. Then he finished packing his brown duffel bag. Then he clipped his nails and shaved his face and enacted all those other mundanities that make a man look respectable. All he had to do next was to not get off the train as it passed the Institute. So he didn't. He didn't get off. He didn't move. He didn't follow. It was one of those odd moments where the most lethargic inaction is the most courageous action of all, or so he thought.

The sun grew high, peaked, lowered. The last few

passengers in his carriage were gone. His body ached with extended inaction.

Time ticked by on the clockless train. It was too dark to read the book he had packed, so he didn't read it. Not that he felt like reading anyway. He just stared at the dregs of the marvellous light which had travelled a billion miles from the sun to the train only to be depleted and dulled by squeezing through grime-grey panels pretending to be windows and then into his imperfect eyes.

It was cold inside the carriage.

The young man stood. Wobbled. Lifted his bag.

He staggered up the moving train and through the final door where a driver was sat in a capsuled tomb panelled with the buttons and levers of a thousand metallic gods. The sacred space was fronted by a large polycarbonate window. The window looked out into the day's hazy remnants of light. The light gave the air in the carriage the impression of a serene sandstorm. Moreover, it was warmer inside the driver's abode; body heat.

"May I sit here?" the young man said, the volume of his voice ill-fitting in that fragile space. The driver was silent, unfazed, irresponsive. The young man sat down, awkwardly, on the only other chair beside the driver's chair, an identical pair. It was oddly comfortable. He laid his hands on his lap as to not meddle with the edges of that electrified coffin, that still space, with the only changes being the flashing of buttons and even those flashes were constant in their regularity. There was a pile of blankets by his feet. He gently pulled one over him. Then the young man said, "What is your name?"

The driver turned towards him and adjusted his own blanket. "You can call me whatever you want." He blinked the stardust out of his eyes and coughed the dust from his throat. "Or you could not call me anything at all. There are only two of us, so I'll always know who you are talking to."

The young man smiled at that logic, a rare smile. "Unless I'm talking to myself," he said.

The driver turned back towards the horizon. "Perhaps talking to others is just another way of talking to oneself." His voice was laced with an unexpected wisdom. And now, he smiled as though he understood what he meant better than the young man did or could.

The young man took a soggy tissue from his jacket pocket and blew his nose noisily. He untied his bow tie and let it hang like a horseshoe around his neck. "How long have you been a driver?"

There was a moment of silence except for the low hum of the space, which the driver's voice somehow merged with, as one, as many. "Years and years," he said. "So long ago that I cannot even remember, like an orphaned child that does not know their own date of birth." The driver cupped his hands together before his mouth and blew a puff of warm condensation. The young man did the same. They shared the warmth they had created.

The driver continued. "Then again, I'm not really a driver, as you say. I'm more of a waiter. I wait, and wait, and in one in a million miles the train will need me – the situation will be so strange and unknown to its mechanical brain that I will have to take over, take hold of the reins and steer us to gentle safety. And so, I wait."

The driver closed his eyes and placed his hands on his lap. "It has never happened before. But one day, perhaps, I will be needed, when my limbs are stiff from lack of practice, when my memories of driving are foggy, and when my reflexes are slow. I will not be able to save us, of course. We will crash and we will die. So I wait and I wait and one day I will be responsible for the deaths of hundreds of passengers, new and old, or perhaps just the death of myself and this money-costing machine called a train, responsible so that those metal algorithms cannot be blamed."

The young man shuddered in his chair. He wondered whether it was because he was cold or scared or both. Probably both. The tomb was silent now and remained so for an innumerable number of indefinite periods of undivided time while darkness slowly swallowed the train in one enormous gulp as it glided along those metal tracks to the sounds of iron insects rubbing their knees together, searching for a mate.

Later, the young man vocalised the melody of words in his music box head. "You are very eloquent, you know. Have you ever considered writing?"

"I've never written a word in my life," the driver said. Then he paused, leant forwards, peered at some dimly lit buttons, and then slumped back down. "But my father always said I had a way with words."

The young man could feel a description coming, so he shuffled deeper into his seat and closed his eyes.

The driver swallowed. "We never knew how old he was, but his face was patterned by wrinkles and whenever you bunched up the skin on his arm it would stretch back so slowly that you questioned whether it was skin at all.

"I remember it was raining one night. It was a dark night, like this one, but with rain. My father wasn't sure whether he wanted to go out into the rain because he knew that he would get wet. But he felt stuck under his shelter as though he was waiting for his own death. So he did step outside. He scrunched up his eyes and clenched his body and waited for the cold droplets to end themselves on his body. But they never did.

"Because a woman with an umbrella had stepped over him. The umbrella covered them both and protected them from the rain. At first, he was confused. But soon he was happy because he was dry and because the woman had smiled at him and because he had smiled back. She was even older than him, if that was possible, and she was so short that her umbrella barely covered his head, but she held it, nonetheless. She held it tightly. I think they're both still alive, somewhere, withering away in bliss." The driver fell silent.

The young man didn't know how to respond, so he didn't. He just thought about something, thoughts not well-formed enough to remember, or express, as he stared into that spotlight darkness, feeling an odd connection with the man beside him, who was also staring into that identical darkness and driving them further into it.

The young man's stomach churned and bubbled and produced a low growling noise. The driver reached down the side of his seat and pulled out a squashed plastic bag, which he tossed onto the young man's lap. When the young man opened the bag, the smell of sugar filled the carriage. "Jam?" he said, before biting into one of the sandwiches. "Thank you. This is delicious."

"You're welcome," said the driver as he leant back in his chair. "What about you? Do you have any stories about your father?"

"I'm not feeling very competent as a storyteller right now. I think that's why this old man sent me here."

The driver chuckled. "Old man huh? I'll have to tell him that."

"Oh. How do you know him?"

"We are good friends. If you can call a man who you know better than yourself a friend."

"How did you meet?"

"He is an old friend. An old, old friend."

And then they waited together and in silence.

At last, the young man fished a small ounce of reality from the puddle at the bottom of his mind. "I meant to ask you – your friend, he told me that you could recommend somewhere to stay in the City."

The driver blinked his eyes closed and then open. "Yes, of course. Well, there are hotels, but you're better off renting a room if you're tight on money. There's a fish and chip shop with a spare room at the moment, which you might want to try." The driver gave him directions to the shop, which the young man visualised and memorised.

When he had done so, he said, "Thank you".

"My pleasure," said the driver.

Later, the young man readjusted himself in his chair. The young man noticed that the dark sea of the horizon was clearer to him now. Hints of definition had started to appear between the analogous expanses of land.

The young man said, "Do you mind if I sleep?"

"Not at all. I might join you," said the driver. He smiled.

The young man pulled his blanket close. Then he rested his head against the shuddering window and his breath began to form a soft and steamy mark. When he arose from his slumber, he remembered staring out into the black pupils of the sky, those holes leading into infinite and empty space. He remembered thinking about the cold air rushing around the train and his own safety from that terrible wind coming out of and disappearing into darkness. He remembered closing his eyes and his consciousness slipping in and out of that same darkness and hearing a mumbling in the seat beside him – a phone call, perhaps, or a fragmented prayer.

Then the young man sat more and stared once more at the ever-alluring horizon. As his eyes slowly adjusted, he could see clearer and clearer the contours of the open land, those vast plains only divided by towering pylons and boundless wires silhouetted against the sky. Soon, dim specs of light became visible from afar, lights marking the tips of tall buildings or dotting the grid-patterned windows of homes, lights made of electricity and power and heat – the lights of the City.

The young man looked over to the driver, his guide, his companion, his newfound co-inhabitant of this inhospitable world. "It's been nice talking to you," he said. "I've not been in a good way lately, so your kindness means a lot. Thank you."

The driver was reclining now, his chair bent backwards as far as the small cabin would allow. "We all get battered and bruised," he said. "It just takes time to learn to cover up our scars."

The young man left the station, his duffel bag patting his leg at every step like an annoyingly affectionate dog as he followed the driver's directions to the fish and chip shop.

The streets of the City were narrow and cobbled and were strewn with the smells of suicide, of screeching cats, of rats skittering out of dark-grey gutters, of strange noises beyond open windows. Occasionally, a car pulled down the road, its fumes thick and black, its lights shining dim through those fumes, its groan filling the too-narrow, too-bumpy street, and fading away again.

But of course, you will know what the City is like, for only the luckiest have not lived there at some point or other. You will know that the young man would have stood out like a blue plaster on a sore thumb all because of his Institute suit as opposed a flat cap and a frayed jumper and worn trousers.

The people passing the young man wore curious, resentful, reverent expressions on their time-slackened faces – faces which brought up memories, mostly bad, some good, all buried, all brown. Some walked around him leaving air to spare. Some stared at him with awe-filled faces. Others breached the gap by firing a dollop of frothing spittle.

A couple others chose to rob him.

He had never felt so defenceless when two metallic men approached him – men with grime on their faces and oil in their hair and each of them wearing a menacing stare. One of the men cracked his knuckles like a nutcracker, one by one, each time with the snap of a walnut splitting in two.

"Give me your bag," the nutcracker man said. His voice was encrusted with dust. He nodded towards the bag and his companion held out a hand patterned with thick, black lines that would make the most cool-headed palm-reader dizzy. The veins on his arms would make a vampire faint. The arms themselves could knock a yeti unconscious.

The young man remained mute. Part of him wanted to suggest that they only took his money and not his entire bag with all his clothes. But the other part of him knew that everything made of matter could be sold to a buyer with shadows on their face and coins in their pocket and faces on those coins. At least his notebook was safe in his pocket.

He handed the bag to the patterned hand.

The nutcracker man looked him up and down. Then they scrounged away to crack more nuts.

The young man stood still. To distract himself from his sorrows, he reflected on how much more lost he now felt even though he was standing in the exact same spot as he had been a few moments before. Then he wondered whether 'to be lost' is a feeling at all.

Then he collected himself. He breathed in a deep breath of sewage and snot and burnt rubber. He adjusted his glasses. He rubbed his eyes. He noticed the blue and yellow sign of the fish and chip shop jutting out from a cracked brick wall. He paced towards it.

Through the glass shopfront he saw a big-bearded man shovelling chips out of a fryer, sprinkling them with salt and vinegar, and wrapping them with dexterity into a paper package along with a battered fish and mushy peas, all while another bearded man was shovelling chips into fryers, removing fish from fryers, and mushing peas. Such was the remarkable and unappreciated symbiosis between these two men. Both were wiping the moisture from their brows with sweat-laden kitchen towels.

The young man entered. A bell jingled. The air was thick with oil and vinegar.

The walls were unplastered, but were mostly covered by various veils: large posters displaying now-exotic fishes; framed photographs of that same street corner but before the Fall with twee horse-drawn carriages and slatted wooden doors; a huge, buzzing box containing bottles letting out a leak of cold air into the otherwise muggy heat. There was even a large pinboard littered with leaflets for various local events and extravagances. At a glance, every leaflet was out of date.

The only other customer left the shop with a jingle and with a paper package cradled in their arms. One of the chip men glanced at the young man and squinted at his suit. The other chip man pulled a large battered fish out of the frier and placed it onto the metal grate behind the acetate barrier.

The first man turned to face him from across that peach plastic counter. His beard looked like it could hide several mice and, beneath his braces, his white vest revealed enough dark armpit hair to hide several more.

"Good morning, Sir." He nodded his head slightly. "What can I do for you today?" He spoke in a falsetto that made the young man wonder whether it was really him speaking at all.

The young man's eyes fell onto the array of fried delicacies and then back to the chip man's untamed, orange eyes. "I'm looking for somewhere to stay. I was told that you have a room free at the moment."

"That's great to hear. You're in the right place, mate. Oi Harry."

The other man, with an identical outfit and body, turned around.

"I told you we'd get a new one soon, didn't I?"

Harry nodded.

The first man turned back around. "How long were you thinking of staying?"

"Only a few nights."

"Oh. I guess that'll do. No one stays anywhere very long these days." He rubbed his greasy hands on an even greasier apron. "I'm Henry, by the way." He extended a veiny arm with a greasy hand on the end and the young man shook it. It was a firm shake. There was a certain strength to it, a certain comfort in the sturdiness of those fingers. It left the young man's hand sticky and moist.

The young man placed the affected body part on the counter for a moment. Then he rubbed his hands together, which miraculously did not cause the grease to disappear, but just spread the stickiness across them both.

He dropped his hands to his sides. He wiped them on his trousers. He cleared a small fly out of his throat. "There's one thing though. I was robbed on the way here. All my money and possessions are gone." On the word 'gone', he held out two empty palms. "And I have no access to money in the City." He dropped his hands back to his sides. "What's the chance that I would still be able to stay here?"

A thick, black line appeared between the chip man's eyebrows. "You want to stay here without paying us?"

"No, no, no." The young man began pacing back and forth, back and forth, parallel to the counter, re- and re- tracing a line on the ground. "Well, not really."

He kept pacing, mind going tick, tick, tock.

"Would I be able to pay you by writing a story, no, several stories, for you, for the shop. They could be about fish and chips. They could be relevant and bespoke to your business."

He kept pacing.

Stopped.

Continued. "They could act as little stories that your customers could read as they wait for their fish and chips to get then stimulated and salivating."

Stopped.

"What do you say?"

The chip man scrunched his brow once more, scrunched it like a piece of paper to be thrown straight into a mesh metal bin. "I'm not sure about that, mate. This isn't a charity."

The young man stepped closer to the counter. "Oh no, this wouldn't be charity, not at all. I should have said– I'm a writer. Yes, a writer. I write stories for a living."

He started tapping his fingers on the table. The speed of his speaking quickened.

"I can assure you, if you give me the chance, that I can write you such good stories that the people who read them in the queue while they wait will be even more likely to come back to the shop. Think of the increase in sales. Look – I could pin them up on that board just here." He turned wildly, pointed, stepped over to the pinboard, and tapped on the cork several times. "What do you say?"

The chip man rubbed his apron again with those hands covered in the juices of fried food, that liquid lotion of his occupation.

"I suppose you work at the Institute for a reason," he said. He turned to his colleague. "What do you think, Harry?"

Harry was silent for an agonising moment. Then he nodded and continued feeding potatoes into a chute while turning a handle that forced them through a sharp metal grid.

Henry turned back around. "Well, the big man has spoken. Sir, it looks like you can stay here. But only for a few nights, at most." He nodded to himself, satisfied with his act of charity that wasn't charity, but kind of was, but also wasn't. Then the chip man said, "Well get writing then. Chop chop!" He laughed at his cooking-related pun.

"Thank you, thank you, thank you," exhaled the young man.

There was a vacant pause, like all pauses, except for the pregnant ones, which are just bursting, ready to pop.

This one didn't pop.

The chip man just said, "You look like you're hungry" and the young man nodded so that his chin hit his neck. "Nothing is free in this world, but I'll give you a portion of chips as part of our deal, how about that? We can't have the Institute on our backs after all!"

Then he scooped a dripping heap of chips from a fryer, wrapped them, and handed over that glorious package to the young man. He took it with outstretched arms. He wanted to hold it close to him. He wanted to cherish the burning heat and let the stench seep into his suit with a perverse sort of glee. But he didn't.

Then the chip man said, "I want a dozen stories by the time the shop opens tomorrow. And source your own paper and stuff. This isn't a charity."

"Yes, of course. I have my notebook. Thank you again, really."

Then his new host nodded to the door at the back of the shop. "Your room is the first on the right, upstairs. There isn't a key. Enjoy." He smiled and the young man smiled back, the warm parcel in his hands.

Filled with fish and chips, for the rest of that evening, the young man didn't stop thinking about what he would write. Images darted in and out of his vision and his mind turned those images into words. He scribbled several short stories that night as neatly as he could without inhibiting his creative flow. He scribbled them into his brown notebook with its scuffed edges, topless, lying on his new bed, facing the window, the light, with his forearm supporting his body until his shoulder began to ache and his clavicle felt like cracking. But that is the sacrifice a writer must make.

Later, he neatly tore out the several stories and pinned them up on the board that would be his outlet. Then he tore out a piece of paper and wrote the title 'Stories for a Chippie' and pinned that up too.

The chip men seemed pleased. He had earned his stay, so far. Here are two of the several stories he wrote that night.

The Potato:

The potato, when he was a young spud, always wanted to grow up and become a chip. He worked hard all through bottom school and got into a well-established top school and it seemed as though all his dreams would come true and that he would finally manage to become the chip that he deserved to be.

There were only three interviews between him and a life of deep-fried prosperity. This was his time to shine in front of the people who would determine his future. But the interviews had many challenges. At the first interview, he had to complete a very difficult test. It was so difficult that our poor potato could not even understand most of the questions. During the second interview, he was tested by the foreboding interviewers once more, through conversation this time. But they befuddled him with their words, and he felt belittled by their superiority.

Yet, despite these adversities, somehow, he got through to the third interview. This was the interview where they were to decide whether he was really cut out for the job. He was given a peeler. And a knife. The peeling was easy, albeit painful. But when he got to the point of chopping himself into those nice little chip-shaped chunks, he found that he couldn't bring himself to do it.

Instead, he had to return home naked and ashamed as the disgrace of his family, the potato who didn't have the starch in his guts to carry out his dreams, dreams that they had supported him with at every roll of the way. Without his skin, our poor potato oxidised: he grew brown and rank. Ashamed to show himself in public, he withered away until his last and uneventful day.

The Homeless Man:
Paul had just got his portion of fish and chips from the local fish and chip shop. He loved fish and chips. He loved the salt; he loved the vinegar; he loved licking the hot, greasy fat off his salty, vinegary fingers.

But as Paul waltzed contentedly down the street, licking his greasy fingers, he came across a homeless man sitting on the sidewalk. Not only this but he glimpsed the homeless man's eyes. He glimpsed their hunger. He saw their sheer jealousy of the chips that he was cradling, relishing, revelling in. He thought that if the homeless man were not so old and weak and tired that he would have grabbed the chips right out of his hands. (Indeed, Paul thought that if the old man were not so weak and tired, he would not be sleeping on the streets at all.)

Now Paul, upon seeing the homeless man's hunger, considered what to do. For some reason, he recalled the old saying: 'If you give a man a fish, you feed him for a day. If you teach a man to fish, you feed him for a lifetime.' Paul thought that it was a very nicely structured and profound saying, so he decided not to give the man his fish or his chips.

Instead, he placed the bag of fish and chips on the curb, just out of reach from the other side of the sidewalk where the homeless man was sprawled. Then he went into a nearby fishing shop, politely asked to borrow a fishing rod, and offered it to the homeless man.

The homeless man snatched it. He held it out so that the end dangled over the bag of chips. After a few concentrated moments, he hooked a chip out of the bag and slowly drew it towards him. As soon as it was in reach, he gobbled it up and reached out with the fishing rod again. This time he managed to hook the entire battered fish – he drew that ketchup-smeared, grease-covered cod towards him.

When he got his hands on it, he tore apart the fish and shoved it into his mouth in huge pieces, barely giving himself time to chew.

He started coughing. No. Choking.

His chest was heaving as though he couldn't breathe. He couldn't breathe. But the heaving soon stopped. His face relaxed. His body slumped down further against the wall and his head hit the ground.

That was when Paul realised that the old saying had turned out to be true, for Paul really had fed this man for the rest of his lifetime.

A few days passed.

The young man had gotten nowhere, idiomatically, although perhaps also physically. Then again, what does 'to get nowhere' really mean?

The morning after his arrival, Henry told him all about his family life including his two lovely children who were stolen by their mother, and about his aspirations to get the 'Best Fish and Chip Shop in the City Award' and how last year the reason they didn't win was because a rat scurried out from behind the counter just as the investigator was leaving.

As more days passed, the young man realised that he was the archetypal fool, the concentrated culmination of every conscious being's understanding of what it means to be gullible and stupid and naïve.

He had spent the previous days walking on water with no glass beneath his feet, not knowing what that metaphor means and why no one believed him when he told them that he was a writer, a professional writer, that his work was valuable and that they urgently needed him.

"Why are you here and not at the Institute?" they would say, and every time the young man didn't have an answer. And so, he walked and strolled and meandered the streets in his dark-grey suit. Asking around, begging, bargaining – to no avail. Job centres. Old placentas. Slowly going mad as he scraped by, living off grease and grime as the days paced by, the days adding up like ones and zeros in a calculator.

The night before his breakdown, he had a dream. He was finding clues to stop a face-sucking, metal-armed creature from destroying his bed and tearing out the soul of his mother.

He woke up laminated in sweat.

Part of him was too worn out to attempt to interpret the dream. Another part of him interpreted it as being the manifestation of some intense anxiety. Perceptive, really. The source of this anxiety was unknown to him. The answer lingered at the back of his tongue. The question occupied more and more of his mental space over those increasingly empty days.

Then, he realised that he had no idea what he was doing in the City in the first place. He realised that he had no money, no direction, no contacts, no contracts – nothing, zilch, the zenith of zero – and that the only reason he'd been able to get the job at the Institute and escape the City was that his parents had conveniently died and had given him their modest leftover winnings from life. He realised that he had only gone and messed everything up with his lack of writing skill. Or, rather, his laughable inability to write anything that anyone wanted to read. He realised that his attempt to fix things by going to the City was but a futile attempt to escape from his horrible failure of a life.

He felt like the potato who had just peeled himself raw but didn't have the bloody guts to follow the thing through. He wondered whether he unconsciously knew that he was the potato when he wrote that horrible story. The answer was maybe, perhaps, mayhaps.

And so, and so, and so, he didn't know whether to go back home to his partner or not. Whether to admit his shame or not. What he would even do then, or not. The same, probably. He would just keep drowning, probably. Not spiralling. Just drowning. Slowly. Silently. Elegantly. Like a slug covered in fine salt as viewed by a hummingbird with its thousand heartbeats per second and diluted perception of time, of change, of swirling matter.

He missed her. His love.

He called her that night, huddled against an unplastered wall with a pinkish tint as the pig-tail wire's rubber coating caressed his arm as it dangled from the cold plastic receiver in his clenched, clammy hand as it rang, and rang, and rang. And stopped ringing.

Sleepless nights. Sleep-spotted days. Grease-sodden chips for breakfast, lunch, dinner. He kept writing stories for the chip men to earn his stay. He had written so many miniature stories that he hoped they would fill up the wall and spill onto the floor and cover his sorrows once and for all. He wondered how long it would be before the chip men kicked their squalid tenant out onto the street with no one left to call, not that he'd ever had anyone to call.

The chip men couldn't understand why the young man would keep paying his fee at the Institute and come to the City, and they watched in bemusement as he came back from his job searches each day more confused about why he was here, there, about what he was doing, what he was thinking by listening to that random old man in that random blue room, while wondering whether he just hadn't listened hard enough, smartly enough, or been good enough.

Then the shower stopped working.

As such, young man stopped showering. As such, he stank. He smelt so rank that noses tightened as they passed him on the street. So rank that his nose had become blind to his rankness. He stopped leaving the shop. There was dirt in his pores. There was grime in his fingernails. There was an inexplicable gunk in the roots of his hair. Stubble had grown all over his face. He was gross.

That was when one of the chip men said, "Christ, if you're a writer but don't want to work for the

Institute, there's always the anti-Institute folks." He sniffed loudly and his beard wobbled. "But I'm not sure that's the kind of work you're looking for."

"Wait, what?" went the young man, or something like that, some bodily expression of interest born through despair. This was in the chip shop, by the way, one morning. Harry was sitting on a corner table in the chippie, counting cash and coins into a tin, the young man still rubbing sleep, smog, and fear from his eyes.

Harry continued speaking as he hypnotically piled up coins into piles. "Yeah, a guy came in here the other day asking who wrote those stories, you know, the ones you did up on the wall. I talked but didn't tell him much. He's interested that you're not at the Institute. Said he had an opportunity. Sounds dodgy to me."

He reached into his pocket. "But I mean, he left a card with his number, if you want it." He handed a card to the young man's surprised fingers. "You might want to give him a ring. Oh, also, we're playing poker here with a couple friends tomorrow night. You're welcome to join us, to make the numbers up. We can lend you money to play. Just try not to be too miserable company."

The young man accepted the invitation with bewildered features. "Oh, I might do. That would be nice."

"All right buddy, now go call your mystery man."

The young man did as he was told.

The pig-tail stretched itself out once more. Clicks of the phone dial. Five rings. Eyes closed.

"Hello. Who is this?"

"I, um – apparently you came to this fish and chip shop and noticed my stories. I think you wanted to talk to me."

"Ahh yes, so you are the fine man I was hoping to meet. Meet me outside that shop of yours in half an hour, if it's not too much an inconvenience."

The young man didn't know what to make of the implication that he had no plans, no other arrangements, nothing better to do. "Okay," he said, through that plastic echo chamber.

"See you in half an hour."

The phone went dead, idiomatically, but not physically, because in case you were not aware, things that are not living cannot die.

Half an hour later, the young man was waiting outside the shop, as instructed.

White gloves approached. A black suit. Pure black; custom. A white bow tie; custom. A black cylindrical stick with a bronze, spherical top, which went tap, tap, tap. Polished shoes, which went tap tap tap. People slouched away from this figure as it traversed the street. Rats scurried off at its passing. The young man just watched.

Then they were next to each other, backs leant against the brick wall with each other, both with one leg crossed over the other, both facing the other side of the street where the man with more face than beard and more sleeping bag than body lay crooked and mangled on the ground. The stick man asked with a voice as clear as water whether this man was the muse for one of the stories on the chip shop wall. The young man nodded.

The stick man tapped his stick against the ground.

"I've often thought it would be a good test of a man's integrity to see whether they could kill one of the homeless. Less affecting than a peer, but still has a certain atrocity about it, don't you think?"

The young man was still. He stared at the pattern of the bricks on the across-the-road wall.

Then the stick man cleared the bubbles from his throat. "I'm going to cut to the point. No funny business. No beating around the bush. Just a plain and frank conversation between two people who can help each other."

He paused, for effect. "Shall we walk?" He pointed his stick down the road.

But the young man replied with a quiet 'no' and the stick man set his stick back down. Then he crossed his arms and let the stick dangle from his gloved hand.

After a brief pause and another coughing of bubbles, the stick man began a monologue during which the young man did not speak. The monologue came forth like a waterfall, which flushed away the sound of all other sounds, sounds which were still there, but hidden. His speech was soothing to the ears but muddling to the mind and the young man could not decide what he thought of it however hard he tried. This was what the stick man said.

"Let me try to convince you of something. I hope you will listen carefully. Because if you want money, if you want lots of money, and if you want money fast, you will want to work for me."

As the stick man spoke, he gauged every dimension of the young man's body language like the measuring stick that he was – and he fitted his slick speech to those exact dimensions.

"If you ever feel uneasy about the morality of working for the Institute, if you have ever recognised the corrupting paradoxes of the system, if you've ever felt guilt for being a cog in a mechanism which drains the life from what you love, you will want to work for me."

He paused, sniffed, and continued.

"If you're sickened by the sight of men and women, young and old, clicking industrial mice connected to guarded screens and typing their identities into reinforced keys on nailed-down keyboards on those brutal, oblong printers that litter these streets, by the sight of them licking their lips with ignorance and bliss as needles churn and groan until a moment later a book pops out like a new-born babe, printed, bound, and packaged in brown paper for that thrilling moment of suspenseful unwrapping, that carefully controlled hormonal kick."

The stick man took out more rulers to measure and fit, small rulers, tall rulers, nice rulers, cruel rulers.

"If you remember the time when you could buy a book that isn't chosen by an algorithm that decides want you want to read, what you want to hear, what will keep you content or submissive or angry, an algorithm that feeds you chicken nuggets that look golden on the outside but on the inside are but gruel that satisfies a person while turning their very mind into that same gruel, an algorithm that knows everything we've bought and consumed and felt and feeds us those same spices to us like a curry of drugs–

The young man didn't remember those times. The young man didn't remember.

"If you are angry that whether a piece of writing is good or bad or not is determined by an underground network coin-counting, number-tracking, story-storing machines that ceaselessly feed stories to helpless blobs of meat, and that any resistance to this Institute cannon is squashed like an ant, an ant without a colony because every ant has already been squashed.

Pause. Measure. Fit.

"If you are all or any of these things, then you should want to work for me."

Shift.

"But only if you are willing to harm a person. Only if you are willing to kill a person. Only if you have the guts inside that fleshy outside layer of yours to set off a bomb inside the Network. Only if you have the guts to destroy countless computers, to maim the Institute, and to cause hundreds of workers to die."

He hit his stick against the hard, grey ground.

"So, do you want to work for me?"

He waited for the young man's eyes to shrink back to their normal size. But they remained as large as an ostrich's eyes even as he staggered away like the flightless bird that he was, away from the stick man and the shop and the street, nearly tripping over his own unpolished shoes on his two-toed feet.

The stick man calmly called after him. "Call me when you change your mind."

Wandering the streets.

Drinking.

Head in the harsh sand.

Shouts.

A brawl.

Maybe him, maybe not – him probably watching like a wimp while downing bartered-for liquid and being snarled at in his decrepit suit.

More drinks.

More shouts.

More brawls.

Blanks and dot-the-dots and spot-the-differences.

Shadows and shiver-inducing sounds.

Somehow, with darkness for light, he found himself banging on the chip shop's door.

He staggered forwards.

Fell back.

A chip man caught him and put him on a chair.

"Mate, mate, are you okay?"

The young man wheezed out a grunt.

A wooden table hit his head.

Oblivion.

It was late the next night and the young man's body ached and the fish and chip shop was made hellish by the dim, red light scattered from the table lamp and refracted in the hazy, red smoke. The perpetual odour of grease and salt was overwhelming, as always. But there was something sweet and dangerous about it now. Sweet like the saccharine smell of stiff paper when one held the cards close to one's face. Sweet like the taste of hard plastic on one's calloused fingertips. Sweet like the stares of those other men with the salty sweat on their hot bodies frozen with concentration.

The men played to the sinister sounds of shuffling and dealing that make the well-conditioned spine shiver. They played to the tune of their precious poker chips pattering on the table intermingled with the pattering of the soft rain outside and the background-score of muffled shouting. The poker chips went click-click-click on the somewhere-in-between-hard-and-soft surface of the red-and-white chequered linoleum tablecloth on a round, flat table, although, then again, all tables are flat.

Ratatat. Ratatat.

One of the chip men kept tossing three navy chips with a flick of his fingers so that they spilled from their stack before stacking them up again, tat-tat-tat, and repeating the action in an endless tease as he waited for the other chip man to knock twice or throw more plastic rounds into the ever-increasing, periodically-swallowed pile of chips. There had been a fourth, perhaps a fifth, but they were long gone, or maybe minutes gone. Who knows.

The conversation was trite and light-hearted. Gossip. Gossip about people the young man didn't know. In-jokes. Banter. Nothing worth putting in a story meant to make people think or enjoy. For no one likes to gossip about people they do not know unless they are born to be outsiders… Henry had lent the young man a fiver. The young man was playing conservatively. Money was not so much at stake but pride. Then again, the money was nice, the illusion that is money, that make-belief, that parameter, unspoken, but agreed, which contributed to the conviction and tension under which they played.

The chip man who had been fidgeting folded. The other chip man took the pot. Probably Henry, maybe Harry. Either way, he was the one who brought up the matter of the stick man, which the young man did not remember telling them about.

"Here's what I don't understand. Why did you come here to earn money if you turned down that man's offer?"

But the prompting was unnecessary. They had already said that he needed to vacate soon. They already knew that he was on the brink of submission, that the stick man's speech had never stopped prodding the fleshy sides of his mind. They knew. They knew. Knew, know, new. Perhaps they also knew that as he stared at those colourful chips sliding back and forth on the chequed tablecloth, he made up his mind.

He didn't know why.

He just did.

He made up his mind. Like make-up. Like he was a notable woman preparing for an notable ball. One that he didn't yet know whether he would regret.

The young man huddled once more next to that unplastered, pinkish wall. The white card was in one shaking hand. The telephone was in his other hand, the handset uncomfortably snug in his palm, the receiver painful against his ear, the buzzing diaphragm uncontrollably loud as it rang and rang and rang. Eight times it rang. It is a desperate man who counts how many times a phone has rung.

It stopped ringing with a click that connected the two participants through the disconnect of space and time.

There was no noise of greeting from the other side. Not a 'hello'. Not a grunt. Not a single sniff. The young man could sense the smug smile on a mouth that knew it didn't need to open, that knew exactly what the caller's next words would be, and that just waited and coaxed and teased the young man to say them without the smallest inkling of a prompt. O how devilishly confident he was, wherever he was, whenever he was, on the other end of that strange connecting aether.

Every second that the young man waited to say what he had promised his desperate self to say was another sliding second of his unforgivingly finite life. Not that anyone was counting. Or cared.

At last, he expressed those chattering words that had already been chattering in his head–

"I'm in. I'll do it."

Then the young man sensed the sly smile thicken and stretch, thick and elastic like putty being pulled by a contortionist with kaleidoscope eyes.

"Meet me outside in half an hour," said the phone an instant before the disconnect tone chimed.

'What was it with this man and half hours?' the young man asked himself. He asked himself a lot of questions in that half hour. He thought the kind of thoughts that don't tell you anything yet tell you everything at the same time, thought that are both a comfort and a terrifying confrontation with the superficiality of reality.

Then the young man wafted his wrinkled jacket and rinsed the grease from his hair and smudged the muck off his shoes with a spittle-wetted thumb. His feeble effort to lessen his decrepitness made him feel even more numb.

Then he waited, and as he waited, he stared out of the window, at the street, at the scene. As the clock's slender finger finished its half-rotation, he saw the stick man approach. The door jingled. He descended the stairs. The stick man held a bag in one hand and no stick in the other and he passed right through the shop and past the young man and up the stairs.

The young man chased him up the stairs and followed him into his own room. He made his bed in a fluster and opened a sweaty window and shoved his notebook into a drawer. The stick man sat down onto the bed with its once-white sheets greyed by lack of affection. Then the stick man placed his bag to the side and rested his hands on his lap. His hands were engulfed by leather snow.

Then he nodded towards the door and the young man closed it. Then he nodded towards the chair and the young man sat in it. Then he nodded towards the curtains and young man reached out to close them but then the stick man shook his head. He nodded again towards the curtains, no, towards the window, and the young man looked out of that low window, looked out at the usual vista. Crumbling homes. A couple of beetle-like cars on a highway littered with drains and debris and despair. Men smoking outside a pungent pub. Girls were giggling as they crossed the gravel asphalt cobblestones. The homeless man was sprawled across the opposite pavement. All was framed by those flimsy, greying curtains, as usual. All usual. The young man was too used to that view by now. Too used.

He felt a tap on his shoulder and jolted. He turned his head and saw what must have been a gun held in the stick man's soft, snowy hand, like an offering, a sharing, a gift. The gun was glistening, black, black as the blackest beetle, black as the blackest, most viscous, most volatile oil.

He stared at the gun pointed towards him, resting on that extended birch branch. It was pointed to his heart. The wind blew and the gun turned one-hundred-and-eighty degrees. It's handle was like an offering, a sacrifice, a gift.

The young man stared at the gun. Then he stared at that dark figure with its black suit, its impeccable hair, its sickening smile, the smile of a rich man who shouldn't be rich smiling at a poor man who should be rich by now, the smile of a corrupt man who felt ever so justified staring at an honest man who felt his guilt as though it was still fresh and fermenting and sodden.

The young man looked at the gun, again. Then at the stick man's face, again. Then out the window, again, at the stick man's face again, out the window, again, at the homeless man, back to the stick man, at his eyes, back at the window and at the homeless man, the more-sleeping-bag-than-man, lying on that opposite pavement, so cosy, so soft, so safe.

The young man was still and static. His mind mined beneath the ground and glimpsed a rocky, golden chunk and then swam back up to the surface. Then the young man breathed out "no" with noxious air into the blackened breeze. He blew another "no" and slowly rocked his head from side to side to side like the softly billowing curtains and blew another "no". Blew it like a bubble into stagnant air.

"Yes," the stick man said. He rocked his head down then up then down.

That was when the young man saw the blank space between the lines between every atom in the universe.

He staggered out of the room. The door slammed. He was shaking. He'd encountered death before. Buckets of it. So many buckets, so many damn buckets. He was still shaking. Bre– bre– breathe–

"Not everyone has what it takes to kill," said the stick man from inside his room. "I need to know that you do." The words floated to the young man's ears. He already knew what the stick man wanted. He already knew why.

He cursed. Swore. He swore more than he ever had before. He swore swear words that he had never even swore before. He swore until he had forgotten how to swear any more. Crescendoing. Diminuendoing. Accelerandoing. Ritardandoing. Breath– breathe– He could see his whole measly life spilt out in front of him. Blocked walls fell and crumbled into sand. Wet sand.

The young man felt sick. So, so sick. So sick that he gagged, that he almost puked up his diet of chips into a salty, soupy mess. But he didn't. He just stood. Shaking. At the top of the stairs, the banister clenched in a vein-patterned fist.

He pressed his other hand against the wall. Support.

He closed his eyes. And breathed. Breathed in. Breathed out. He repositioned himself, back against the wall and slowly slid down it. He touched his face. It was still there. Touched his eyes and ears and mouth. They were still there. He grabbed his forehead by the temples with a tensed hand. He opened his eyes, his hand shading them from the harsh, synthetic light. He stared, into the space, into the light. The light stared into the holes in his eyes. The peeling walls were inside his body.

The shadows penetrated him.

He wondered what the homeless man was thinking about right now. He wondered what the homeless man had eaten for breakfast today. He wondered how long the homeless man would take to die if the young man did not do what he was about to do. Not that that's how causality works. Then again, some things happen whether you want them to or not.

Then again,

Then again,

Then again, the young man was enough of a man admit that it was of his own volition that he went back into his room and took the gun from the stick man's hand and walked down those steps knowing exactly what he was going to and why he wanted to do it.

He crossed the shop and went out onto the road and across the road to where he knew that rotting figure to be. His mind told him all the desperate arguments that desperate men and women and children use to justify the most desperate actions. It told him that we are all just made of atoms, that atoms don't feel pain, that atoms don't suffer. It told him that we are all made of nothing but organs and tissues and cells and organelles and molecules and proteins and atoms. Because it's hard to empathise with atoms. Because they're so inconceivably different to us. Because they're so un-visualisable by their very nature. But they are what we are and what we always will be – matter, forces, energy. And so one part of him screamed "are you made of atoms?" and the other part of him screamed "yes".

Bang.

I know onomatopoeia is cliché, but hey.

Blood dribbled from the homeless man's forehead.

He staggered back across the road, through the shop, witnessed the fear in the chip men's eyes, fell up the stairs, collapsed into his room and dropped the hot-cold gun on the wood-boarded ground. He squinted like a baby held up to the sun.

The stick man didn't blink, like a lizard.

The young man must have closed his, or turned around, or left the room for a second, for a moment, because when he opened his eyes, or looked around, or came back in again, the stick man was gone, must have slipped, skidded, slimed out like the well-dressed, gelatinous fish that he was.

The young man crumpled down onto his crumpled bed. It groaned under his weight and he groaned back.

They groaned together. Time passed, as it does. The young man probably had a nap after that. He probably had a nap.

Later, he felt angry for being so pathetic about the whole affair. Angry that he hadn't been more of a man about it all. Angry that the world let him suffer so terribly while letting him know that he was so terribly lucky. Angry that the word 'angry' suddenly seemed appropriate to use, in his head, in his mind, when he'd never needed that word before, never believed in it, that concept before, in the days when he had more, and thought he had less, control.

He woke up again and this time the sky was dusk. He sat up and noticed that his notebook was on the desk and was opened onto a page which was filled with writing that wasn't his own.

He reached out, grabbed the notebook, slumped back down, and glared at the neat and swooping writing.

The bomb is inside the jacket. Use your status as an Institute client to get into the Network for a tour. Navigate to the section that matches people to books.

Once you have activated the bomb, you will have five minutes to exit the building. A car will be waiting for you outside. The driver will hand you the money and drive you to the station. It is in our interest that you survive and are paid in full.

Rest up. You'll need it.

And remember, subtlety is the weak man's weapon.

That was when he saw that in the corner of the room lay a dark-grey suit, a red bowtie, and a pair of pointed black shoes. Institute attire. New Institute attire.

The suit-jacket was heavy. There was a button with a safety guard under the collar. He didn't have to guess what the button did.

Under the jacket was a shaving kit. He heard rushing of water. He rushed to the bathroom. Water was pouring forth from the shower. It was as though every mythical monsoon story had suddenly come true.

He shaved his face free. He showered and scrubbed himself free. He dried himself free with a plump towel. He shoved his old clothes down hard into the bin and admired his new clothes and went to bed naked.

He couldn't stop thinking about how easy terrorism is. The young man slept like an insomniac that night.

In the morning, the young man walked to the entrance of the Network. Everyone knew where the entrance to the Network was. It was the heart of the City; it was the brain of the City.

As he walked, he received no more animosity than red-eyed stares and maniac chuckles. As he walked, his feet hurt.

He arrived.

Imagine a concrete square amongst piles of bricks, a smooth square, just there, in the middle of everywhere.

Enter.

Imagine Hall Two without the chairs or the stage, and smaller, and filled with those hip-high, weighted pillars connected by elastic strips to form an intricate labyrinth. Imagine lots of marble desks and shiny barriers and signs signalling different sections of the Network.

The young man joined a queue. But it was a long

queue and he was wearing a suit so he strode right up to the front and placed his hand on the reader.

There was an amber ding.

"Please state your reason for entry," a nearby desk woman said with a voice as sour as nectar as she adjusted the thin grey glasses on her nose and looked down at him.

The young man summoned the courage and cocky confidence of every admirable man he had ever known or met or seen. He summoned their auras. He needed them now, needed their energy. He ran his newly-cleaned fingers through his newly-cleaned hair.

"I'm here for a tour."

The desk woman clicked her computer and, a few moments later, the barrier opened. "Enjoy your tour."

He didn't seem to need the charm. He walked through the now-open barrier. His heavy jacket felt light on his shoulders.

He met a man labelled Eighty-Three on the other side of the barrier, a short man who compensated for his height by standing with very upright posture and by wearing shoes with a thick slab of rubber at the bottom such that they elevated him off the ground.

Near the end of his tour, the young man asked where they kept the computers which matched people to books. Eight-Three took him there.

Then the young man took off his jacket and flicked up the safety barrier and pressed the button with a wince. He shoved the jacket into a bin's gaping mouth.

When Eighty-Three commented, "Weren't you wearing a jacket?", the young man said "No", and so Eighty-Three was content.

Then the young man said he urgently had to leave. Eighty-Three took him up the lift and to the entrance and he walked swiftly out of the guarded door.

He saw a single black car at the corner of the road, buzzing with stifled life. He approached, made eye contact with the driver through the tainted open window, and got inside. The window closed. The figure in the driver's seat said "Done?" and the young man nodded.

They drove away, slowly, in silence, one mind chattering, the other chewing. When they felt their seats shake and heard their seatbelts jitter, when they saw the ground wobble and they could smell smoke, the woman handed him a briefcase. He opened it. He looked at it. Money.

Soon the car pulled up at the station and the young man got onto the train.

The train journey passed like the blink of an eye looking out from within a black hole.

Then the young man was leaving the station, again, his station, a station. He was walking through the gate, again, his gate, a gate, to the woods, the nicest route, the quietest route. He walked in the direction of that pale orb in the sky which some people call the moon.

He hugged his money-brimming briefcase against his body – squeezed it so tightly that it merged with him, became one with him.

Then he shook it in the air, showing it off to the world, to the woods, to the woodlice. He struggled to stop himself from whooping aloud like a howling monkey, like a howling gibbon with gibbous eyes and a reverberating throat – like a monkey finding a mate and shouting, screaming 'look at me', 'look at me', 'look at my blue bottom', 'look how loud I am', 'look how proud I am'.

He was practically running, running forwards, with his briefcase in one hand and with the fingers of his other hand tapping the trunks of trees as he practically ran past them such that grubs came to the surface of that rough bark that he didn't even need to eat. He clutched and swung off branches when he could have used his feet. He jumped over rotting logs and kicked up leaves with his money-brimming briefcase in one hand and the other hand free–

He grabbed a handful of orange berries and tore them from their stems and threw them upwards and forwards and laughed as they hit him on their descent. There juice on his hand, in his hair, lichen beneath his fingernails, soil on his face, on his shoes.

Finally, he left that area of glorious rot and wandered out into that complex of crystal-cut concrete, one of many and yet so unique.

The ding of the reader became a melody in his head. His footsteps became percussion to this melody. His briefcase bumped his leg with affection upon every anticipatory step.

As he put his hand on the reader to the door to his home, he called out to his love, "Darling, darling" with a grin contorting the skin on his face.

She didn't answer.

Ding ding. Both blue. No one else was home. The door opened. He stepped inside.

"Darling?"

He turned the hallway light on. Her pair of shoes were gone.

Blink.

He looked at the hook–

Her coat was not on the hook. He looked away and then looked back quick hoping he had mistook the first look that he had took but the first look was not mistook. The clock went tick, tick, tock.

Blink.

He paced into the kitchen. Blink. Light switch. Paper. Paper on table. Folded paper. Why was there folded paper on the table–

Blink.

He placed down his briefcase, gently, carefully, slowly. He reached out to the paper, took it, unfolded it, looked at it–

Dear beloved,

I have been thinking about things since you left. I've had lots of thoughts. I've probably had a week's worth of thoughts in only a few days, if that.

I did once love you. I used to passionately love you. If I am remembering things right. I used to love you with the adoration of… I never did have your way with words. Maybe your way with words was why I loved you so much.

I have been thinking about how I changed my life for you. It's odd because it felt like I was changing it for myself. I might have been. But it also might have been that I loved you too much. Or maybe I didn't love you enough. I don't know. Maybe you loved me so much that you couldn't see that it was not me who you loved after all. If that makes sense.

But it was fun while it lasted. I hope you would agree. The days we spent with each other were nice. And the days we spent apart were nice. I have many beautiful memories of our time together. I hope that you do too. Do you remember when we first met under that bridge and just stared and smiled at each other? Just smiled! I think about that moment a lot. Do you remember how you always used to buy me flowers and pretend you had gone out of your way to pick them? It was so obvious. But I never told you so. Even though you knew that I knew you were lying. If that makes sense.

You always liked to observe things. I mean tiny things that other people didn't notice. Or if they did notice that they didn't think about, or maybe didn't care about. I think you would put them in your stories. Perhaps that is why your stories never sold. I like to think that things you noticed about me are in some of your stories too. But maybe not.

I'm undecided whether moving to the Institute was the best or worst decision of my life. It made you happy. That's for sure. Probably because you felt like you had a purpose. I think you thought your work was finally getting out into the world and you liked the fact that it would have your name on the front in big letters saying, 'look at me', 'look at me', 'remember me'. It definitely made me happy to see you happy. But slaving away at the school all day did not make me happy. Maybe, if I could, I should have become a writer like you.

I think that's everything I wanted to say. Sorry for not returning your calls. It was too painful to speak to you once I had already made up my mind. But I wrote this letter to tell you that I am leaving you. I already filled out the de-relationship form on the printer. When you read this letter, I will have already left. That's if you do come back and read it. I think I've just always wanted something different from life than you. And I think that your goals have become incompatible with my heart.

I have to stop writing now because I am getting the train to the City. I hope it does not hurt you to say that I hope to meet another man. I hope we can find somewhere other than the Institute or the City to live, if that is possible. Please don't find the courage in your heart to try to find me. Then again, I shouldn't worry, for I do not yet know where I will end up myself, only that I am going to find another.

Yours faithfully,

Jane.

Breathe, deep breath, the young man taking back in the air that he had slowly exhaled as he stared into those words on that malevolent page. He read it once, skimming with large saccades. Then read it again, eyes hovering on every word. Then he looked at the blank spaces between the words, between every line. He looked at the first letter of each word, of every other word, of every sentence, paragraph, trying to remember the secret codes he had read about in detective books, hoping that there would be some kind of sign that it was all a cruel joke. He rearranged the letters of the words in his head, scrambling, scrambling for an alternate meaning… He found nothing but nonsense. Nothing but anagrams for those same malevolent words.

The letter dropped from his fingers like a petal from a fatly blossoming tree. It fell in cascading arcs like a fragile feather from a bird being ripped into pieces.

He kicked the table leg.

Slammed his fist–

Down.

On the table. On the hard, flat table, on the calm, white doves on a calm, blue sky. He grabbed the tablecloth and tore it off and threw it across the room. It collapsed softly in the corner. He grabbed the briefcase and threw it across the room where it smashed a stock ceramic ornament and clattered to the ground. He sat and slammed his head against the hard, wooden table and sobbed like a man who had forgotten how to be a man.

It would not have been surprising if in that moment he had stood up and turned on the kitchen hob and clutched the counter on both sides of the stove and pulled himself into the burning gas of those scorching rings, for the heat to conduct down his body and turn his bowtie into flame and turn his shirt into a white, dripping candle and to make his belt ash, trousers soot, socks cinders, shoes tar, for the flames to envelop him, swallow him, re-mould him.

He wanted to sweat like a foetus in a boiling womb.

But he didn't.

He didn't.

He was just…

Still.

Still, while the curtains billowed like mournful whales from stories he'd read about the sea.

He shot up and his chair clattered back and he picked up the table with monstrous hands and flipped it across the room.

Glass smashed.

He wiped the tears from his eyes and blinked three times–

Footsteps.

The footsteps were made by a man with close-cropped hair who had got into the building and into his home and whose blue jacket bulged over his muscular frame as he grabbed the young man's arms and pulled them taught behind his body like a blue chameleon's tongue securing its fluttering prey.

He struggled.

His oppressor took his wrists with one monstrous hand and hit him with the other.

He kicked.

He wriggled.

He writhed.

"Help!"

His oppressor hit him.

"Help!"

He hit him again.

And again.

And again.

The young man stopped wriggling.

The oppressor began to drag him out of the open door.

Stairs. Corridor.

It was dark outside now and the complex of window-dotted dominoes was shrouded in a sudden gloom. The oppressor dragged him to the platform.

People stared at his restrained and mangled figure, wondering what evil he had done and what his deserved fate would be – sticking their noses in his business, lapping up the sweet nectar of his pain for their own satisfaction, the satisfaction that they weren't him and he wasn't them who was being commandeered by a wretched blue-jacket – that catharsis of pity and fear.

The train arrived.

The doors opened.

The oppressor pushed him over the gap and held him with his back to a slimy, yellow pole and clamped his arms behind it.

That was when the young man realised that he was in the carriage that he always avoided in case it was the same train as the one he was on when he had been shoved into that cold, hanging body with its rubber, teardrop necklace limp and swaying in time with the chugging of the juggernaut train, its swaying, swinging, feet dangling, tiptoes barely grazing the tacky ground, its face puffy and bulging, dead.

Memories.

Images.

Molecular circuits.

He remembered how he had stood there, done nothing, been nothing, been witness to nothing – not the ring on her finger, not the tip of her swollen tongue peering from between purple lips, not the clammy mist of her grey and gelatinous eyes like a fish on ice, not the note in her pocket, not the ripples of her scarlet skin where the yellow rubber had suffocated her neck.

He remembered pressing a button, a red button. Or did he? No alarm went off. But at the next station, men in blue jackets sifted in and snipped her necklace and rolled her body away. Gone. And as he stared at that swaying, useless necklace now, he wondered how the woman had managed to fit her head inside it at all. The more he thought, the more he remembered not having done anything at all, that he had just staggered away and spat phlegm onto the hot-cold ground like the disgusting creature he was and watched as blue-bottles swarmed the platform with their shiny, navy overalls sealed by ocean-black gloves and ocean-black boots, ocean-black, ocean-black, ocean-black.

The train doors opened.

He was dragged down the long, wide road.

He was dragged past the revolving doors. A blue-jacket handed the oppressor a linen bag.

Darkness. The rustling of dusty fibres. The swoosh of displaced air. Tight, tight pain against flesh and tendons where the string was pulled taught above the collarbone and below the jaw in that convenient area in between. Small strands of frayed cloth filled his nostrils. Dust was his hair. Stale residue collected at the back of his mouth. Grimy sourness. Sapping moisture. Closed eyes, damp, irritated. His few square centimetres of atmosphere were wet with bacterial droplets from sneezing and sneezing and sneezing until a force from beyond his senses hit him.

He stopped sneezing.

Tried to stop being. Awaited suffocation. Waited to see where he would be taken. Fear, vehement fear.

It's an odd feeling, being dragged blind down corridors along with hundreds of others who are dragging themselves and being not quite sure who is dragging you, one person or more or perhaps the entire tide of others, that great slug of bodies with its rippling crawl.

For a moment the young man was weightless. Then his nose was full of dust and his mouth was ringing and there was the feel of warm blood on his face. Bodies flowed past him, around him, over him. Pressure on his back, dirtying him, suffocating him. Pressure on his arm, twisting, reeling. He tried to stand up but bodies were everywhere and bodies were all. He felt his white shirt being printed with the soles of a thousand strangers. Then his arm was grabbed and nearly pulled out of its socket and he was standing. Then he was being shoved forwards again, regained balance again, and all would have been forgotten were it not for the pain.

Down, down, down, his feet barely catching himself as he fell forwards, an action not like walking at all, the way an animal walks, mindless, instinctive, every step a new realisation of how close its body is from smacking against the ground.

It got quieter the further down they went, if he could trust that gravity was not playing tricks on his floating mind. So quiet. Just him and his oppressor, he hoped. There was something nice about the idea the same one had followed the job through.

He entered a room.

He wondered what makes a room a room. Maybe it's the echo. Echo.

The bag was untied and grabbed and tugged off but his surroundings were just as dark as before such that he felt rather than saw the hard chair being pressed against him, the rope being tied around each of his lims, the scrunched cloth being crammed into his mouth.

He didn't mind the darkness. He was done with seeing anymore. But he still struggled. He struggled with the valouor of a medieval knight and the futility of a three-toed sloth. His oppressor hit him. He stopped.

Footsteps.

A closing door.

The scraping of a lock.

He screamed "Help!" Not that he knew who he hoped would save him. Besides, it turns out that you cannot scream "Help!" when there is a cloth inside your mouth. The scream came out muted and muffled, followed by a guttural choke and a gasping for air and when the air didn't come the sound of sucking it up through his nose as though snorkelling in a sea of the stuff, that inaccessible dread. Ahhhhhhhh! He shook his wrists and his feet in their bonds but the knots did their job and they did it well. He was still breathing pathetically up through his nose and every few seconds he was swallowing the saliva that built up at the back of his throat.

Time passed. Passed out. Passed past. Passed around. As it does. As time passed, it slowed down, or sped up, or both. Or at least, his perception of time varied in this vicissitudinous way, oscillating like a resonating string or a bouncing ball or a falling feather's gentle arcs, because, of course, time, in reality, is constant as long as the Sun circles the Earth in its indefatigable, monotonous perpetuity – and it is only in the mind that it bends like a flexible ruler or putty in warm hands: sticky, slimy and elastic.

Regardless, the room stayed as still as silence as the however-much-time whittled by, only measurable by the nagging hunger in his gut and by the vultures pecking at his soul.

He heard footsteps.

The room was lit up with bright light that blinded him even more than the darkness had done.

He waited until his eyes stopped hyperventilating.

Then he saw a now-closed, white door separating two white walls beneath a panel of white light. On the right was a white table beneath a dark-grey computer and keyboard and mouse. In the middle, against the door, a tall man in a lab coat leant.

The young man gasped. Then choked. Then coughed. Gasped at the man in a lab coat, at his towering form, at his thin physique, at the so-smooth skin like the skin of an egg on his face, a face so barren of expression that it might as well have had no features at all and which gave the impression that any slight force where his nose should be would cause a stream of albumen to come rushing forth followed by one whole gelatinous yolk that would splat against the ground and form a gluey wet heap like the expelled placenta of an elephant alongside a scattering of shattered shell.

The young man did not move, so filled and frothing as he was with fear and fatigue and fascination.

Not only this, but the whole body of this strange man gave an impression of fragility: his long, white lab coat looked like it was made of porcelain; his long, white legs seemed rigid and stiff and wobbled at the knee; his smooth, white boots performed a queer clink on the ground as he un-leant himself, stepped closer to the young man, and then sat down on the table.

As he did, he reached with the spidery fingers of a gloved hand into the large side pocket of his lab coat and retrieved a small, silver, cylindrical object which tapered at the top, like a pen, which was a pen, which he spun between his fingers. He clicked the pen such that an inky point emerged from its tip.

The porcelain man clicked the silver cylinder again, threw it into a small bin in the corner of the room, whooped as it went in, and then turned back to the young man with his faceless face.

"I didn't need to do that," he said. Then he sniffed loudly and adjusted himself on the table, both legs dangling and swaying out of phase but at a steady and satisfying frequency. The young man watched from the side as those white legs scissored hypnotically back and forth. Then they stopped still. "It was intimidating though, wasn't it?"

Then he took a yellow boiled sweet from his pocket, unwrapped it, and popped it into his mouth.

Immediately, he crunched, sucked forcefully with his cheeks vacuumed in, and then crunched again.

"Anyways," he said, still crunching, "I presume you know what this is about, what you're here for, and all that jazz." With a slender finger, he picked a piece of hardened sugar from his upper left molar and ate it.

Then he turned to the computer, clicked and shuffled and scrolled a few times, and then said, "I've got your file up here." He muttered some personal details as if to prove that fact. Then he said, "Have you ever thought about how the word 'file' has multiple meanings? How cool is that?"

The young man nodded, nodded a small nod, tied up as he was, humbled by his blood-stained face and his torn-up trousers and his sole-stamped shirt with its bow-tie collar. He was like a clown. Like a clown from one of those books. Like a clown with all the horror knocked out of him.

The porcelain man continued clicking and shuffling and scrolling and demonstrating his expert control over that electrical mechanism. "We better cut to the chase, I guess. You are suspected of planting a bomb in the Network. You destroyed quite a lot of stuff. I'll spare you the details. But it's going to be a real pain to replace."

He rolled his sweet wrapper into a tight ball, aimed it at the bin, and then threw. It went in. There was no celebration this time. "Pretty horrible thing to do, I must say. Although we all have our reasons, I guess."

He was staring straight into the young man's sodden and traumatised eyes. "Can you confirm the truth of this suspicion?"

There was a short and silent performance where the porcelain man pretended to not know why his interviewee wasn't answering. Then he opened his eyes wide with mock-realisation, chuckled, leant over, and then tugged the gag out of the young man's mouth.

The young man waited a moment for this thing called moisture to re-experience his mouth.

Then, finally, he spoke.

"I – yes. I did it."

The porcelain man nodded. "Well, that was easy. I mean, we knew you did it anyway, but are you sure you don't want to put up a little more resistance?"

The young man remained silent as the other man popped another skilfully-unwrapped peppermint into his mouth. He didn't crunch for a while this time. He just sucked out all those herby synthetic juices – every last drop. Then he said, "While we're at it, can you explain the series of events leading up to your attack?"

The young man flinched at the word 'attack'. Not that it wasn't true. Not that he wasn't a murderer with a sandy, slime-covered pebble for a heart. But the young man collected himself. He thought for a while. He thought and then he told the porcelain man everything that he knew. He told him about the stick man who scouted him and about the fish and chip men who gave him a room and about the nutcracker men who stole his bag and about the train driver who directed him to the chip shop and about the old man who directed him to the train driver and about Brian who directed him to the old man.

All those so-close memories felt so distant now, so out of place, as though they were no longer his own. It all felt too convenient, too perfect, the chain of events too well-oiled.

The porcelain man was still, the gloop in his head stirring, whirling. He asked for more details, specifics, you know, and the young man gave them, all of them.

That was when the young man felt that he had earned the right to ask, that he had a chance. He pushed his throbbing shoulders back. He tried to shake the hair from his eyes. "Would I be able to put in a request?"

The porcelain man scoffed – nearly choked on another boiled sweet. "You realise that's not how this works. There's a very unequal power dynamic here." Crunch. "Possibly the most unequal power dynamic of all."

The young man replied as quickly as he could without seeming too desperate or afraid. "Yes, yes, I know. And I did what I did and you know what I did and you've got me. You've got me good and proper. I know the consequences. I know the deal. I know how this cruel world works. I just – there's something I want to ask, that I need to ask, something that I need to request. Can I put in a request?"

The porcelain man had moved to a previously-unnoticed white office chair and was spinning on it. "We don't take requests. You're a criminal."

"Who decides who's a criminal and who's – no, it doesn't matter." The young man tried to find the porcelain man's eyes. "Please. Please. It's a small request. A very small request. Will you–" The young man stopped himself, slumped himself, hearing himself.

But when he didn't continue, the porcelain man nodded, such is the curiosity that kills even the most powerful of cats. "Yes?"

The young man looked at his own reflection in those porcelain eyes. "Will you let me write a story? One last story?"

The porcelain man saw no reflection in the young man's dull, gelatinous eyes. "Your status at the Institute has been revoked."

But there was a fine inside those gelatinous eyes. "Yes, of course, but you could make an exception. It would be easy for you, surely, to make an exception, powerful as you are." The flames danced in the air as though to perform for the man who held his fate in his palm, the crinkled wrapper of a long-gone sweet. "Just one more story. One last story. Please. It's what I live for."

The porcelain man stopped spinning. "Okay. Yeah, why not?" He smiled. "What can I say? I'm a nice guy.

Think of it as the last nice thing anyone will ever do for you. But, if you deceive me, I will kill you." He laughed.

And the young man laughed too, a quick laugh, a short laugh. The porcelain man manoeuvred the mouse for a while. Then he turned the screen around so that it faced the young man. Then he pulled a large, white knife from his large, white pocket and cut the ropes around the young man's cramped hands and raw wrists.

The young man began to type.

The porcelain man watched him for a while, then he cut the ropes around the young man's feet, left the room, and locked the door behind him with a clink.

As the porcelain man left, he kept typing. After the porcelain man left, he kept typing. The porcelain man's footsteps became distant memories. He kept typing.

He typed and the pads of his fingers wore thin and purple with bruises. He typed and his ears went numb to the rat-a-tat-tat of the plastic keys, in and out, in and out, in and out. He was like a spider weaving an intricate web, I suppose, one of creativity, one of language, one of hope, one of knowledge. But so too was he the fly fluttering into this invisible-yet-o-so-visible web, trapped by its sticky strands, and wriggling to escape only to be drawn further inside by wrapping itself in more and more sticky, silver strands.

But it wasn't too late.

He stopped wriggling.

He relaxed.

He typed.

He typed and he felt the tug of hunger at war inside of him, and so he chewed the air. He typed and his eyeballs began to ache with pain, and so he closed his eyes. Salty water dripped from the corners of those eyes. He kept typing. It ran down his cheeks and dripped off his chin. He kept typing.

He typed and the images that he described lit up the stage in his mind and he gave them life.

At last, he got to where he is now, typing the words as he lives them, as he keeps typing, keeps typing these words now, nonsense, filler… as he stalls as he waits for the porcelain man to return, stalls because he fears that if his fingers stop moving for one moment that they will never start up again and that the story will never be finished, his story, the story, and so he shouts "I'm done!" and he keeps typing and he shouts "Come back! You said you'd come back! My time is up!" and he keeps typing.

The porcelain opens the door and comes in at last.

"Hello hello." He closes the door, swaggers over, and props himself up on the table. "Oh, before I forget, we followed up on those people you mentioned, you know, this Brian and all the other men."

The young man didn't have anything to say to that, so he just kept typing, kept typing, waiting for the porcelain man to finish his pause–

"Yeah, there's nothing much to say about it really. Just that we have no client named Brain at the Institute, that room numbered 6899 has been unoccupied for weeks, and that train you got to the City has long been fully automated. Oh, and that there is no fish and chip in that part of the City. In other words, either you're deluded or a liar or a pawn with a cranium filled with candy floss. Strawberry. Maybe vanilla."

The young man typed as he experienced the tingling sensation of realising that his entire understanding of people and kindness and trust and lies had been realigned. It was, was like watching the world wiggle into a thousand fragments of glass and dust. He didn't really feel like typing anymore, didn't want to move his fingers, didn't want to think, live, breathe anymore. But he did. He did. Because he wasn't yet done and he couldn't stop now, couldn't not not not not finish now–

Not.

The porcelain man was silent, unphased, irresponsive. Thoughtful, even. The young man hated that fact. He hated him and he hated himself and he hated everything else such that there was nothing else to hate no more.

"Well, it was nice knowing you," the porcelain man said.

The young man felt as though everyone in the world

was polishing tin. But he collected himself, yknow. He collected all of his scattered pieces and held them back together with an army of trembling hands. And he said, he said, "Thank you. I am nearly done, nearly finished with my story." Then he said, "I just need one last thing. I just need you to tell me…" But voice tapered off and these words are filler for until he picks up his stream of thought once more. Then he said, "Please can you tell me, how will I die? I need to know. I need you to tell me. I need to finish the story. Please tell me so that I can finish my story."

The porcelain man grinned a grinny grin made up of a million smaller grins. "I cannot tell you that," he said, said, said. "You've been allowed enough luxuries already."

The young man didn't hear him. The young man wasn't humbled. He just paused and let the sombre air ring and let a tantalising soup of sympathy bubble up and boil through the softness with which he said, "Please tell me. I need to finish my story."

Pause.

"I cannot–"

"Then give me five more minutes."

"I can't– "

"I said, please, okay, I said, please, okay, it's been days, days and days, so many darn days and now all I ask for is five more minutes, how much is it to ask for five more minutes–"

"This isn't a chari–"

"I said give me five more minutes!" Ring. Silence. He said those words like an animal about to die.

Pause.

Perhaps the young man will be grabbed by the hair – no, by the arm. Almost certainly. I will be dragged down white corridors, white, white corridors, and then into a room, where I will be shoved and backed up against a wall, most likely, yes, and the porcelain man, no, another man, a man with a gun, a shining black gun, will hold it up to my face – yes – and he will aim, will look at me through some small slit or some small eyepiece but he will not look me in the eye, and he will shoot, and I will hear a noise, a digadigadiga or a tttttttttt or some such noise, and there will be a ripping pain, yes, a ripping pain – a ripping pain? – yes, a ripping pain in my chest, in my breast, with each rusted, silver bullet tearing my tissue, piercing my organs, bursting my brain, perhaps, yes, yes, and then I'll collapse and the world will go black.

Blood will be seeping from my body and into my clothes even as they pick me up, shove me into some makeshift coffin and into an incinerator, probably, and they will close the coffin door and the incinerator will be lit and the porcelain man will watch, yes, and maybe mutter a prayer – because he does have a conscience really, guilt, yes, yes – and I will be engulfed in flames, although he won't be able to see my body melt, yes, and then my body will turn to smoke and ash and heat and will drift up out through some funnel outside and will dissipate into the sky, into the air, into the wind, and I will both be gone and present at the same time, different, I suppose.

Or perhaps I am wrong, and I will be buried. Maybe, actually, yes, worms and woodlice and fungi and bacteria and other critters will eat through my coffin, and they'll encroach on me, crawl over me, digest me, slowly, although not too slowly, dissolve me, turn me into food, then excrement, mix me into the soil, and plants will grow in me, and I will be a new source of life, yes, I would like that, and I would be gone, but still be there, I'd be different, yes, I would like that.

Acknowledgements: Thank you to all to my English teachers at Kingsdale Foundation School who have encouraged my writing, especially to Gabriella Dawson for encouraging me to enter short story competitions back in Year 11 and to Alec Hutchinson for being the first to read this when I hadn't told anyone else about it, for showing me that publishing is possible, and for being a constant source of advice. Otherwise, thank you, Sebastian Warren, for being a thoughtful friend and talking with me about all things creative. Thank you, Tamsin Pierce, for caring about me and for helping me be less unhealthily obsessive when writing. Thank you, Mum and Dad, for being being so patient and for encouraging me to get this story out into the world. Thank you, everyone else who read and commented on this manuscript: Andrea Varney, Anne Eggbert, Ben Snowdon, Hester Schofield, Louis Upshal, Richard Cannitcott, and Susan Wilcox. In fact, thank you to everyone who I have talked with about this project in any shape or form because every ounce of interest and praise and feedback is what turns a bunch of words into, well, a finished bunch of words. Lastly, thank you, reader, for taking the time to digest these words and for hopefully getting something out of them. If you did, please consider giving this book a review on Amazon. Your thoughts would be greatly appreciated. Lastly, I hope you pass this book on to someone you think will like it because, after all, words are meant to be read.

Printed in Great Britain
by Amazon

20571730R00072